THREE (

THE WARRIORS

A Warrior triumphs
from darkness to
light & discovers
God's **purpose**
for his life.

Christian Claudio

christianclaudio.com

DEDICATION

I dedicate this book to the source of my all, my family Angie, Sebastian, and Brooklyn.

I want to thank my best friend and amazing wife, Angie Claudio. What can I say, honey? What an amazing ride this has been. I am so grateful that Father God has trusted me enough that He gave me the privilege to be the husband of His precious daughter. Because when it is all said and done, remember you are His favorite! Your beauty inside and out knows no bounds. Your heart is literally made of gold. Your mind is set on our King, and your eyes are continually looking to see opportunities to serve the less fortunate. You are a strong negotiator when managing our home and making space to focus on my career and projects. I love how you created an inviting atmosphere of warmth and love for our family and friends in our home. I love how you use your gifting of hospitality to minister to those around you. I have never seen someone work so diligently to complete all that God has laid upon your heart. And you never spend time dwelling on those things that do not please our Lord. And best of all, you are the mommy to our two precious champion kiddos. I adore you so much.

To my Warrior son Sebastian, you are my firstborn, my little leader. From the first I laid eyes on you; I knew of the champion you were to become. There were many times the Lord would use you to speak wisdom to your momma and me. One of those times I am so grateful for was when I was at my significantly worse moments as a father and husband, as a seven-year-old, and from the heart of God, you looked up at me and declared, "I have no peace in this house!". Those seven words cut to my soul and were one of the monuments I thank the Lord for when He showed and spoke through you. Now, as you grow into the Godly man you are destined to become, I am blown away by how amazing you are. It is not just as a brother, a son, or as an athlete, or a student, or as a friend but as a man. As you get closer to the next phase of life, always remember that you were set apart for God-given greatness. Your assigned purpose for the Kingdom is world-changing; you carry the anointing of General Joshua. Your leadership, creativity, and strength will be used to lead and take territory for the King. Your momma, sissy, and I could not be prouder of you. You have done well, son. We love and appreciate you.

To my Warrior princess, Brooklyn. We are so enamored by your beauty. In fact, while mommy was pregnant, Sebastian, who was three years old, showed us a picture of a model in a magazine. The young girl had brown wavy hair and blue/green/grey eyes. Your bubba pointed to the image and said, "my sissy." Every day your mommy and I are still blown away by how you look so much like that picture. But what's even better is that you are so incredibly gorgeous inside your heart too. You are a worshiper of Jesus, your photographic memory continues to blow us away, and your wisdom is way beyond your years. My favorite "God-moment" with you was after my second hip replacement surgery in 2017. I was sitting on the couch in the living room, and my soul was not in a good place. I needed encouragement in a big way, but I kept it to myself. Praise and worship music was playing, and you began to praise the Lord. First softly, then boldly. So powerful, in fact, I was caught in the Spirit and began to praise Him too! You led me in praising Jesus for what seemed like minutes but was close to an hour. My spirit soared, and I was blown away. You continue to blossom as an incredible young lady. I am so proud to be your daddy and am blown away that the Lord chose me for you. Your heart is pure gold, you have the anointing of Queen Esther, and you are destined to bring peace, justice, and favor to those around you and be an advisor to Kings. You are a gem in our eye, baby girl. Your bubba, mommy, and I love and cherish you so much. We are so very proud of you, honey.

FOREWARD

I first met Christian Claudio in a large meeting room at a local hotel. It was July of 2011, and we were in the early phases of planting a church that God commissioned my wife and me to establish.

Christian was a young husband and father of two wonderful elementary age children. Little did I know that his marriage was in a fragile state, and there was chaos inside his home that he was in no way proud of, yet he was searching for answers. He loved God, and he knew that Jesus was his Lord, but he did not learn how to overcome the battle within his soul and his four walls. Fortunately, he soon got the breakthrough he needed that only Jesus can provide, and freedom came to life, his marriage, and his family.

Since that time, which has been almost ten years, I have been able to see Christian on fire for God and evangelizing on the college campus. I have seen him feeding the poor and consistently hitting the city streets of a metroplex, searching for homeless people to share the love of God with, and provide food and clothing for them. I have watched him function in church leadership and discipleship of other people, young and old.

I have been able to witness Christian's entrepreneurial side as he has grown in the business world, where he has had significant success and influence as a businessman. I have watched him grow as a husband and father, to represent the very person that he represents (Jesus Christ) to his family. I have watched him overcome extraordinary trials relative to his injuries that required hip replacement, followed by another gruesome hip replacement. In his overcoming, he always did it with joy on his face and joy in his soul. I have watched him fight with great warfare for the health of his family as he stood by his wife and warred for her during a life-threatening illness.

Christian is battle-tested. Christian Claudio is a Warrior, a fighter. He has fought many battles in the flesh. He has many scars that are only visible through his testimony and the stories that he can tell. He is now whole, and in his wholeness, he has a story to tell. Christian has also fought many battles in the spiritual realm and has become an expert in both arenas. He is a very gifted man in many areas, one of which is his writing ability. God gave Christian a message, and in his quest to be an obedient son, he embarked upon completing this great work. Because it was inspired by our Creator, it is creative. Because our Creator inspired it, it has a transformational message within it.

I have been an avid reader since 1999, and my book collection has exceeded well over 1,000 books over the years. However, out of all my books, I only have about two or three novels. I tend only to enjoy leadership books, non-fiction books, biographies, and personal growth books. In other words, I do not gravitate towards fictional, conversational stories. Admittedly, upon receiving Three Chambers, I was less than thrilled plowing through the manuscript. I was mistaken, to say the least.

As I began to read Christian's book, I could not put it down. I read this book in one sitting! I was hooked after the first few pages. I was captivated by the characters and their personas. I was utterly caught up in the story, and I could not leave the story until I read through to the end. I was utterly blown away by the end of the book, and I could not help but wonder how my good friend could come up with a story such as this. I quickly realized that our magnificent Creator genuinely inspired him. I am grateful for Christian's obedience to complete this God-given assignment.

I hope that you are prepared to be touched in a special way. I do not doubt that many of you reading this book are in a place in life where you have seen beautiful glimpses of your whole life's puzzle, yet somewhere along the way, solutions seemed to escape you. Or, for some, you just haven't been able to quite put all the pieces together. I am here to bring you good news! Three Chambers is going to steal your heart for a moment, and it very well may provide you with a crucial puzzle piece that spurs you on to completion.

There are not many greater feelings than the feeling of *breakthrough*. God has used my good friend, Christian Claudio, to bring *breakthroughs* to thousands of people who have been searching for a significant piece of life's puzzle packaged as several *aha moments* in your journey through Three Chambers. So, relax and get prepared to go on your personal quest in the pages of this book. Discover for yourself what God has been preparing for you all your life. Embrace the adventure that you are about to embark upon. And lastly, take joy in your imagination racing as you comb through the pages of this epic story.

Danny McDaniel, Founding Pastor and Entrepreneur
Author of - *Power: To Change Your World & Freedom: Winning the Battle Within*

ACKNOWLEDGMENTS

My Confession

To the reader - I cannot begin my acknowledgments without my full confession of the source of Three Chambers. I did not write this book! Ok, I may be one for theatrics, I technically "penned" this manuscript, but the Lord is 100% responsible for the story, characters, and inspiration. I was granted the privilege of stewarding this work of art and bringing it to the world. Those that know me to know that I am not a novelist. Rightfully so, I am not. So, it was only by the grace of God, and the divine appoints I experienced in finding Abigail, Tim, and Jason that this book came about. So, what you love about Three Chambers, well, that is what the Lord inspired. And what you don't love about it, well, that part was probably me.

Lord - I cannot begin to thank you for trusting me with this story. I love you and honor you. Thank you for your love, wisdom, strength, and continued direction in my life. Thank you for your protection, thank you for meetings in your Throne Room, and thank you for Your Kingdom come!

Your son, your Warrior. Christian (the other donkey)

My Scribe - Abigail Gilbert

Abigail was my scribe who mentored me in bringing my story, my notes, sermons, scriptures, dictation, and these characters to life. She tested every word I said and brought it back to the Lord. In fact, how I was able to write this novel was next to miraculous. I would go to prayer and was given a chapter a week. I would then have a weekly call with Abigail and tell her the story, provide the back-drop framing whether it is aspects of the military, behind scene details of the world of MMA, or the scriptural foundations that framed up Eli's journey as a whole. Abigail and her husband Colton would take the work back to the Lord in prayer in final preparation for the conversion from story to novel. Then I would re-submit what was rewritten by Abigail back to the Lord for His final approval. We did this weekly. 14 weeks and 14 chapters later, and Three Chambers was complete. Final edits were done in a similar format. I would then submit the entire book to the Lord with the full understanding it could be thrown out. He then gave me more layers of Biblical truth to layer on top that both added immediate practical application for the reader as well as the deeper revelation that would require Biblical research.

Abigail was literally a Godsend. She is a true professional in every sense of the word, and I cannot begin to express my appreciation for her guidance and mentorship. She was able to take my story and turn it into a masterpiece. Thank you, Abigail and Colton, truly blessed that the Lord chose you both for this project.

My Illustrator - Tim Heron

Tim is an amazingly gifted Illustrator and Graphic Designer. When I discovered Tim, this young man immediately impressed me. Not just by his illustration talent but also by his love for the Lord. When learning about my interest in hiring him for Three Chambers, he asked for the manuscript and read the book in its entirety without solicitation. Which, of course, instantly showed his devotion to the project. With this inspiration, he produced the images that you see on the cover and in the book.

Tim, you are a joy to work with. Thank you for your patience with me and your ability to take words and convert them to an artistic moment in time. You are an undiscovered talent who will see a tremendous amount of success as your career blossoms.

With the utmost respect and admiration, Christian

My Partners - Danny McDaniels, John Caruthers, Eric Jones, Joe Navarro, Tim Bazor, Carmen Medina, Eric Yeager, Mike Mayberry, Kimberly Parker, McKenzie Croy

I am so grateful to all of you. Your commitment to the project and your personal friends is so appreciated. Thank you for taking time out of your busy lives to devote to completing the manuscript review and providing the critical feedback needed to ensure I somehow made the work less relatable to the reader. Thank you for your prayers for the project and the ministry to follow, for your commitment to our time frames, and for your overall love of the story itself. I hoped you enjoyed your gift.

Your brother in Him,

Christian Claudio

Table of Contents

Chapter One

Returning Home

Eli pulled up outside the diner on his Sand Dune Gray Soft-tail, the deep-throated rumble dying off as he cut the engine out front and shoved the keys into the pocket of his leather jacket. He opened the glass door and stood for a moment in the doorway as he always did, scanning.

He wondered what it was like for other people, all those oblivious citizens who walked through doorways blithely and didn't fear what was on the other side. For him, even quiet country diners held the fragrance of his past: the noise from the kitchen like the rattle of gunfire against a Humvee, the man in the corner a potential threat behind his copy of the Daily, the woman with the child possible collateral damage.

He knew it was illogical, that they were all just dropping in for their morning coffee and a bite, that the threats weren't real, and yet he couldn't switch off that part of his life. Kandahar still clung to him. His fingers moved at his side, stretching out straight and then snapping into a fist again. It was a coping mechanism he'd learned over the years--a way to remind himself of the mat, the place where he always felt the most grounded.

The bell clanged as the door shut behind him. In the corner, the man lowered his paper's edge for an instant and then disappeared behind it again.

"Feel free to sit wherever, hon'. Just you?" The waitress was young and tired, her hair swept up haphazardly. Eli did a mental double-take when she whipped the pad out of her apron pocket, feeling foolish when he realized how harmless it was.

"My friend should be here any minute. Coffee, black if you don't mind?"

"You got it, dear. I'll keep an eye out for him. Nice bike." She flashed a quick smile, put the pad away, and left in search of coffee.

He looked out the window. He had chosen a seat in the corner of the diner, his back against a wall, his eyes on the rattling kitchen, and the door that kept opening and shutting for customers to come in. There were two kids bent over pancakes in the booth beside him, earphones in, music leaking out. It sounded like a pop song of some sort, clangy and unfamiliar.

A friend. That's what he had told the waitress, and yet the man he was planning to meet was practically a stranger to him. They had grown up together, shared the same blood, the same parents, the same childhood, and yet he still felt uncomfortable around his little brother. He had only agreed to see him because the phone calls kept coming, and he knew they would persist until he showed his family that he was okay, that this most recent tour was no different than the others, that he was healthy and whole.

The bell dinged again. This time Daniel appeared in the doorway. Spotting Eli, he began striding across the room towards him.

"Eli," his brother called out, opening his arms even as Eli stood to shake his hand. "You're a sight for sore eyes."

2

They hugged, but only briefly. Eli thought how healthy and happy his brother looked. Daniel had grown a beard, filled out a little in the shoulders, and now stood before him smiling in his easy, charismatic way. The brothers were only two years apart, but Eli knew he looked far older than Daniel.

"You should have let me meet you at the base," Daniel said. "Mary and the little guy wanted to be there; you should see how big Jeffery is. He misses his uncle."

"I saw pictures," Eli said with a shrug. "I didn't want you all caught up in the homecoming. It's always so loud and confusing with the families there, and you've welcomed me home before--nothing you haven't seen in the past."

"Well, there was you," Daniel pointed out with a smile. "I haven't seen you." He sat back, crossing his arms across his chest. "You look strong, Eli. Still fighting?" He winked. "I know, I know--you call it rolling, right?"

Eli saw Daniel's eyes flit to the side of his head for a moment and knew that his brother was looking at his marbled ears, "cauliflower" that gave away his preferred destresser.

"There's a gym here in town," Eli answered. "Connected with the owner two weeks ago."

"When you got back?" Daniel asked quietly.

"No need to wait," Eli replied. He couldn't explain the need for one-on-one competition, how his body ached for the power of grappling or sinking in a gogoplata, his guard high and his shin against the throat of an opponent. He didn't mind the pain that came with fighting. It was a black-and-white world where mistakes were punished swiftly, and there was just enough justice to make the world habitable for the day. Eli was introduced to jiu-jitsu before his last tour and had kept up his practice overseas. It did not take the place of his other addictions exactly but held a position of prominence.

The man in the corner of the diner stood up suddenly from the table. Eli's head jerked up unconsciously, and he felt his hand move to his hip. He realized what he'd done too late. Daniel was already looking at him with a furrow in his brow. Eli hated how his family did that--pretending they weren't worried but watching him out of the corner of their eye as though they expected him to implode. He was foolish when he was younger, not so good at pretending, and his family had worried about the things he had seen, the pain he had felt, and the people, well, the people he had killed. Now Eli knew better, and he answered Daniel's questions in an even voice.

"The gym's just something to pass the time," he laughed. "You should have seen my place, though. The sublet left it a wreck. I'll have to clean it up eventually." It was Eli's best attempt at changing the subject.

The waitress returned with two mugs of coffee. "I thought you'd want some," she said, smiling at Daniel.

He nodded. "Thank you. We'll both take the house breakfast." He looked up at Eli. "How do you like your eggs?"

"Over easy."

"You heard the man," Daniel said. "And sunny side up for me."

She nodded, scribbled in the pad again, and disappeared from the table. Daniel took a deep breath and leaned forward, his palms flat on the table as though he was preparing to give one of his pulpit sermons.

"Is this really your last tour?" he asked. "You know you've said that before."

"It's the last." Eli cleared his throat, trying to push back the memory that always rose to the surface when he thought about his reasons for leaving, Charlie's cold, pale skin and staring eyes that were void of movement. He shook his head to clear it. "You know I never meant to make it a career; the opportunities were just too good to pass up."

That was only partly true. The real reason he had returned again and again was the same reason he was worried about adjusting to life without the military: he didn't know if he was good for anything else.

He had earned his Ranger tab and made it through Green Beret training years ago. He'd learned Pashto and Persian and earned his qualifications as a scout, sniper, and combat tracker. He'd known what to do and what to be when he was in the military, and life made sense then. He made sense then. Now, he felt like an odd object, fashioned for a very particular task and, without that task, not at all useful. He probably would have stayed in the force forever if it weren't for losing Charlie, his spotter, and his mentor.

"What are you going to do?" Daniel asked as though reading his thoughts.

"Do you know any desk jobs that require hand-to-hand combat skills?" Eli joked in response. "But really, I have a few openings in the finance sector, and I'm going to an interview tomorrow. They love vets."

Daniel looked surprised. "The finance sector?"

"I have to use that college degree for something," Eli took a sip of the coffee, winced, and dumped two creamers into it to mask the burned flavor. "It will give me a chance to live that normal life you and Mary perfected. I'll find myself a sweet girl and settle down--white picket-fence and all that."

Even as the words came out of his mouth, Eli felt his heart revolt against it all. He desperately wanted that security, the lasting love of a good woman, the chance to pass on his legacy to some rowdy children. Still, he was also terrified of losing himself in that world. He stretched his fingers under the table, made the fist.

He had a nagging feeling that there was something more he was meant to do. It was the reason he had signed up for army ROTC while in college. He had felt then that he wanted to tap into some incredible calling. Yet, after ten years of training and battle, he felt no closer to that elusive purpose.

"Mary and I have been worried about you," Daniel said. He gave a gentle smile. "I know you hate to hear that."

"There's no need to worry," Eli said quickly.

"After what happened--"

"We don't need to do this," Eli interrupted him, waving his hands. "I'd rather we didn't talk about it."

Daniel looked as if he still wanted to share something, but instead, he raised his hands in quiet surrender. "There's no pressure," he said, "but we're going to have a special skit at church this Sunday, and Jeffrey is in it. You being there would be a huge surprise for him, and Mary would love to see you too."

He tossed the comment in just as the steaming plates of food landed between them. Eli knew that he was reluctant to bring up his congregation.

"No, of course, man," he reassured him. "I'll be there. You know I want to see the little man, and Mary too." He jerked a finger up towards Heaven. "The Old Man kept an eye on me while I was overseas, and the least I can do is drop in and pay him a visit now that I'm home."

"'The Old Man' is not only in a church, you know," Daniel began, but Eli waved it away.

"I know, I know," he said. "Of course not."

The conversation was careful after that, even strained. Eli loved his brother, as he knew he ought, but he also knew Daniel could never fully understand his history. He knew that his family tried--Daniel most of all, and his mother before she passed away. He was almost grateful his father had run away when he was a boy: family could be a crushing force even when they meant to do good. Charlie had been like a father, but then Charlie had gone away too. Even God, who Daniel claimed had filled that void, had abandoned Eli.

They were halfway through the meal when a man came into the diner and approached their table. Eli watched him come, nodding to Daniel to alert them that they had a visitor. He was a mountain of a man, possibly a powerlifter, with meaty hands and a cut jaw. Daniel waved him over to the table.

"You know him?" Eli asked in a low voice.

"I do," Daniel said with a quick smile. "I told him to drop by a little later, so I could introduce you."

"This is the first you've spoken of it," Eli said carefully.

The man stopped at the table, clearing his throat. "Daniel?" He was waiting to be introduced.

Daniel slid over. "Sit, Eric. This is my brother Eli."

Eric extended his hand, his tone gruff. "Eric."

"And you are…?" Eli asked, growing annoyed.

"Eric works with veterans just like yourself," Daniel said quickly. "He goes to the church, and I thought he might be a good connection for you now that you're home for good."

Eli was instantly defensive. He had been to therapists before and had sat through his share of well-meaning luncheons hosted by people who wanted to croon over the boys overseas. They were the sort of people who liked the uniform and were eternally "grateful" for his service but didn't want to hear real stories about what he had seen and done.

"Good for you, Eric," he said, unable to keep the sarcasm out of his tone.

"Eric, tell him a little about what your organization does," Daniel pressed, his voice unusually upbeat.

Eric turned calmly to Eli. "I work with wounded warriors, helping to provide support for veterans returning to civilian life."

Eli lifted a hand to flag down the waitress. "Check, please," he said. She hurried off to fetch it. He turned back, ignoring the disappointment on Daniel's face. "Well, I wish you the best with that, Eric."

Eric's stiff jaw worked for a moment, and then he said gruffly, "You know, Eli, I'm a former army man myself. I know the drill. If you're not interested in the organization, I'm not going to shove it down your throat."

"Interested?" Eli raised his hands, palms upright, and gave a forced laugh. "Gentlemen, I'm in the best shape of my life. I don't think I qualify for any wounded Warrior project."

"You might be able to help others," Daniel said quietly. "And there are injuries that aren't so obvious, Eli."

"Which is it?" Eli asked. The waitress handed him the receipt. He briefly looked at it and then pulled out some cash and laid it in the center of the table before standing up. "Am I so wounded I need help, or so healthy I can provide help to others?" He shook his head. "Look, I know you mean well, and I don't want to give offense, but it's just not my sort of thing."

He stood up out of the booth. Eric watched him silently, and Daniel looked down at his hands. Eli thought of the gym, where the guys beat up themselves and others to get rid of the kind of aggression that coursed through his veins. He tightened his hand into a fist again. "I have everything handled."

Chapter Two

Without Purpose

The sun was only just climbing over the horizon when Eli left the mat and began packing up his equipment. He'd already been at the gym for two hours. He preferred the early mornings. This was the time that reminded him of the days before he'd left the service two years prior. He didn't sleep much anyway these days and might as well be putting all those wakeful hours to some use.

Unlike some of his buddies who had left the service and turned soft and comfortable, Eli had hardened in the two years since he'd left the service. He rose quickly in the jiu-jitsu gym, already a black-belt, and gained a sort of grudging respect from the younger fighters. His friends teased him about how much time he spent fighting, leaving his beautiful wife at home every day to get beat up on the mat, but he brushed off their comments. He told himself that he wasn't neglecting Sarah--in fact, he was trying to preserve their marriage.

He felt like a ticking time bomb, his heart screwed up tight in his chest, his mind was always whirring faster and faster at the sights and sounds that reminded him of the war. He didn't want that time bomb to go off on his wife, and so he came here again and again and left the aggression on the mat.

He zipped his bag closed, tuning in to the conversation on the other side of the gym. A few men from his grappling class talked about the line-up for The Galaxy Hotel's upcoming fight. Pólemos Fighting Championships chose this venue to showcase all the up and coming fighters in the region. PFC was the leading feeder organization for amateur and pro fighters who wanted to advance their careers to get to the big show. Eli's gym was one of the top MMA gyms in the area. They had a few fighters on the card, as always.

Eli listened intently as three of the men looked over the paper hanging on a bulletin board beside the gym owner's door. He kept his head down but heard what he had been expecting to hear--an exclamation of surprise and his name.

"Wait, El--" a man named Dre, the most charismatic of the group, called out across the room. "Since when are you on the card?"

Eli raised his head slowly. "Since a few days ago," he answered. He wasn't much for talking, and the other men in the gym knew it. There was respect between them all, but in general, that did not extend to Eli's casual conversation. He made it clear that he wanted to come and work, keep his head down, and avoid friendships.

Dre led the other two men across the floor, a frown on his face. "I thought Dimitri was going up against Draxler."

It was the main event for the amateurs, the winner between the two would get his pro card, and there was quite a bit of buzz about Dimitri when the line-up was first announced five weeks prior. Draxler was a formidable opponent, only one amateur win away from a pro career, a striker with a barbarian's persona out for blood. Dimitri was the favorite in Eli's gym, partly because he was the gym's alpha, partly because he was a well-rounded fighter with high-level situational awareness. He was the underdog, but fighters loved an underdog. It was Dimitri's time.

"Dimitri's out," Eli said quietly. "Tore his meniscus."

The little guy behind Dre, a jiu-jitsu aficionado nicknamed Mighty Mouse, nodded with sudden understanding. "I saw the injury, but I didn't know it was as bad as all that. He spared with someone from the striking class and went down hard, but I didn't think it was that big of a setback. Just ice and rest, and he'd be back on the mat."

"Draxler would have been the end of him anyway," Dre said drily. He turned to Eli. "So, Dimitri is off, but that doesn't explain why you're facing Draxler. This is your first card."

"It's an amateur fight," Eli answered, his head down.

"No fight against Draxler is an amateur fight," Isaac followed up with a hoarse laugh. "The man's already earned his pro status in every way but one--the paperwork. He's not going to hit any lighter before he signs on the dotted line; you can count on that."

Eli set his bag down and crossed his arms. "Coach wanted a grappler," he said quietly, referring to the gym owner. "He spoke to Mick from PFC and asked if I was up for the challenge. They want to mix up the styles in the match."

"It's not unheard of," Dre said slowly, "but you're not ready, man. You've no experience. What does Sarah think of this?"

"I've been working with Coach on striking defense," Eli said, avoiding the question about Sarah. Sarah didn't know, and she didn't need to know.

"Which was what, a few days ago?" Mighty Mouse laughed. He was a striker with cauliflower ears and a jaw of steel, and his eyebrow arched in doubt. "You've slacked off striking since you've been here. Sure, I wouldn't want you to take me to the ground, but you'd have a hard time getting me there in the first place. You're too loose with your chin; you're going to get caught when you try to go to the ground."

"Come now," Dre said, his eyes on Eli's. "Coach wouldn't have chosen him if he didn't see something in him."

The three men nodded, and Eli knew what they were thinking: some of these men had seen the dark edge he worked so hard to conceal outside the gym. Eli knew it would come out at times while grappling with them. A tangible presence of rage would appear without provoking. Even when Coach would say, "just roll, go easy, work countering each counter," but instead, Eli would demand his training partners to tap, stopping the flow of the training session's purpose. It was the reason men like him-- without experience and not well-rounded--would get "the nod" last-minute: call it initiation or call it being thrown "to the wolves" whatever the motive or Eli's flaws, he would make for a good show because of the willingness to go to the deep-end, recklessly.

"You're a strange one, Eli," Isaac said.

"If you want to work on tucking that chin, I'll meet with you tomorrow," Dre said.

Eli shouldered his gym bag and nodded politely to the men. "The striker class will be enough, I'm sure," he said. "See you on the mat."

He turned and walked out into the crisp morning air. Something about the conversation had reminded him of Charlie, and he had a bitter taste in his mouth.

It had been years since he'd allowed himself to think about the man who had first called him into the world of jujitsu, but this morning, Eli couldn't help remembering him. Charlie, who had introduced him to the ring and the mat, Charlie, who had treated him like a son, Charlie, who had been a Warrior himself all those years and had been the image of all Eli wanted to be.

Charlie, who Eli had found slumped over in his office, two days after the team had returned from their last tour, with enough painkillers to kill a full-grown bear.

Afterward, Eli heard people everywhere hypothesizing about the reasons behind the suicide. The note only apologized, had not explained. Eli saw firsthand how desperate survivors are to find a reason for the tragedy and loss of suicide--as though knowing why will somehow make everything right again.

Charlie's absence left a gaping hole in Eli's life. It was the reason he had not renewed his contract, it was the reason he had chosen the little white house with the picket-fence life, and, most notably, it was the reason he had agreed when Matt asked him to open for the pro fight. He knew it was a bad idea--that Sarah would never be okay with it--but his mind screamed yes as soon as he heard the invitation. It was the next level of intensity, a hit of the drug that would last longer than a few turns around the mat.

In the beginning, the fighting had helped to fill the hole. Still, it seemed that every passing day that void grew more extensive, and these days Eli fought a dull panic in his chest--panic that resulted in outbursts of anger entirely out of his control. He hid it from Sarah for the most part, but he didn't know when he would slip, and he could see that if something didn't change, he would ruin the life he had built.

The drive home was always too short. He pulled into his driveway and felt the sweat in his palms, nervous, new sweat from his memories of Charlie. He walked inside and smelled coffee in the kitchen.

Flashing back, it had been two years since that conversation with Daniel in the diner: two years, one wedding, one house on Maple Street, two upward moves in management, and a three-car garage. He rounded the corner and saw Sarah sitting at a stool near the bar, a mug of coffee in her hand, already dressed in her church clothes. Sunday. It was Sundays when Eli felt the most like an outsider to the world created for himself, this beautiful, picture-perfect world. During the day, he almost forgot about his life before. It was only at night that the sandy deserts came back into his memory in short bursts of light and gunfire. Then he would wake up in the night, sweating, praying Sarah had slept through his restlessness, and he would remember how strange he felt in the paradise he'd created.

Sarah looked up from the copy of her latest *Lisa Bevere* book with a quizzical smile.

***

"We have to leave in ten minutes," she said, standing up and tugging at his gym shirt teasingly. "This would certainly make an impact in the front pew. I was worried there for a moment that you wouldn't make it."

He sighed, ran his fingers through his hair. "I was thinking about staying home today; the lawn's looking a little long."

She frowned. "Are you feeling okay?"

He knew why she asked. Since they'd been dating, they'd gone to church every Sunday, like clockwork. She had taken up teaching Sunday school once a month. They got together regularly with Daniel and Mary and Jeffrey. They were part of the community.

***

Eli didn't know how to explain it to her: how strange he still felt in his skin. In the pew, listening to sermons beside all those clean people in collared shirts with their bibles tucked beneath their arms, he was struck every Sunday by how confident everyone seemed. They all looked as though they belonged, as though they knew their purpose, and he felt the contrast to his situation with every passing week. In the pew, the hole seemed to grow larger and larger, and he couldn't keep back the feeling that he didn't fit, that he would never work, that all these people seemed to be whole and full of something beautiful that he didn't have.

"I just don't feel like church this morning," he said after a moment.

"Church isn't about feeling," she began. He cleared his throat.

"Sarah, I believe in God--you know that, and He knows that. I don't think He'll mind if I take a few days off, and I don't think he would appreciate legalism." He knew he'd spoken harshly, but he couldn't pull out of his head. He poured a cup of coffee, watching the brown liquid swirl and fill the black mug in his hand.

She waited a moment before responding. She was good at that: taking a breath before lashing out in defense when he got sharp and uneasy like this.

"Eli, I don't care for legalism any more than you do. You know that. I just know that you need a community around you, and it's moments like these--when you most want to be alone mowing your lawn--that you should go and be around other people." She shrugged. "Who knows, maybe Daniel will have something brilliant to share this morning."

"I don't want to fight." He took a few half-hearted sips out of the mug and then went back upstairs and changed into slacks and a dress shirt.

As they drove the few minutes to the church parking lot, he thought about those words and realized how false they were: I don't want to fight. But he did want to fight, desperately, just not with her. He missed having a battle, a daily calling that kept him out of the mundane, kept him living in the moment. He remembered the feeling of adrenaline with a faraway longing, the power that he'd had when his finger was on the trigger, the control over his own destiny.

They parked and walked inside. He could feel Sarah watching him, worried. There had been no real resolution to their conflict, and he knew it bothered her. There were donuts and coffee inside, and people mingling about sharing the details of their week, passing babies from one to another, and hugging each other with that quick embrace and hearty, "Good morning, brother, good to see you, sister," that Eli couldn't decide if he liked or despised.

He took a seat in a pew close to the back, and Sarah slipped in quietly beside him after a few pleasantries. It was a chapel of sorts, large enough to hold a hundred people or so, with stained glass windows. Still, beyond that, the classical influence fled—a small drum set at the church's front, a guitar stand, and a keyboard. Daniel liked to keep the worship long and the sermon short.

The music started, and Eli stood along with the others to mouth the word s to the songs. He had long ago stopped listening to the meaning of the words. He kept his head back and his eyes closed, but he thought of nothing at all. He spent so much time keeping the explosions out of his mind that he had perfected the mental blank slate. Imagining a blank piece of paper and erasing the blue lines.

He opened his eyes when the songs ended and sat down with the rest of the congregation. Ahead of him on the low stage, he saw Daniel climb up. As always, his younger brother paused for a long moment at the front of the room before speaking, running his eyes along with the familiar faces of his flock with a tender look in his eyes. Only Daniel could have engaged in such a long silence without any hint of awkward shifting in the pews.

"Good morning," he said at last.

"Good morning," the congregation echoed.

"Today, I would like to talk about adventure," Daniel began, drumming his hands against the edge of the pulpit. "Almost every Sunday, I speak of love and acceptance and peace from this pulpit, and I believe all those things to be close to the heart of God, but let us not forget that we are living in the middle of a grand adventure, a battle."

Eli blinked. He fixed his eyes on his brother, but Daniel was not looking at him. He was flipping through his Bible and gesturing to the congregation. "You know the verse," he said with a smile. "'Our struggle is not against flesh and blood, but against the rulers, against the authorities, against the powers of this dark world and the spiritual forces of evil in the heavenly realms.'" He looked up with a smile. "I know just last week our Sunday school teachers taught about them afterward, and my littlest was running around with a cardboard sword strapped to his waist for days afterward."

There was a small ripple of laughter in the room.

"When we are children, it's easy to embrace the adventure of our Father," Daniel went on. "We study about the great heroes of old, and we see that Jesus himself was an exciting man. He was compassionate and kind, but he was also brave and, at times, filled with righteous anger. When we are children, the sword is strapped to our side because we have not yet learned that the world doesn't think it's of any use." Eli knew from his childhood and the last few years at Sarah's side that Daniel was making an illusion to the verse in Ephesians where the Word of God was compared to a sword.

"Then we grow up," Daniel said with a smile. "We learn that our coworkers feel more comfortable if we keep our faith to ourselves, that to everyone else peace means quiet and ease in the background, that our dorm room wall provokes less controversy if we take down that picture of the footsteps of the faith that our grandma sent us." At this last example, he winked towards the back of the room, where Eli knew a few young men from the local university always sat. Another laugh rippled.

"But we were made for more than that." Daniel's voice grew more serious, armor more intent. He leaned forward, his hands clutching the edge of the pulpit. "Don't you feel it? Don't you feel that you have a greater call on you, pulling you to a life of purpose, a life fully lived in the power of your Savior? Even the things we speak about every week, the love and the peace, are powerful. They are not mantras to be worn on your t-shirt or phrases to be thrown out half-heartedly when a loved one is going through a time of trauma. They move mountains, and they should be treated with respect. Without them, there is a void in us that cannot be filled."

Eli had never heard his brother speak like this before. His sermons always seemed simple and to the point, with the occasional untapped insight, but something different about today. He felt the hair on his arms stand up.

"Turn with me to Matthew 7," Daniel said. "We're going to talk about what our lives should look like in the service of this adventure because we have to be rooted in the right things to weather that sort of excitement and, at times, fear." He slid his finger down the page and began to read. "This is Jesus speaking: 'Everyone who hears my teaching and applies it to his life can be compared to a wise man who built his house on an unshakable foundation. When the rains fell, and the flood came, with fierce winds beating upon his house, it stood firm because of its strong foundation.'" He looked up. "You may have heard this spoken of as a 'rock' in other translations. Let's read on: 'But everyone who hears my teaching and does not apply it to his life can be compared to a foolish man who built his house on sand. When it rained and rained, and the flood came, with wind and waves beating upon his house, it collapsed and was swept away.'"

"So, what does this mean?" Daniel asked. There was a long silence, and then he came around the pulpit and pointed into the front row. "No. I get tired of speaking up here all the time. What does this mean?"

This was new. Everything about this was new. Despite himself, Eli sat up a little straighter. One of the elders in the church's front, a short, kindly-faced man with neat grey hair, cleared his throat, and answered.

"We must be rooted in Jesus, the rock, to live through the storms of life."

Daniel nodded. "Yes, John, and I am going to add to that. We've been talking about adventure, and who, in their heart of hearts, doesn't hope for an adventure? I know that even the most proper and correct among you long for something to fight for, whether it's in your marriage or your family or your work. It's how we're wired. But I would add that to face that adventure, we need to have our houses built on something lasting that will not be swept away. If you want to fulfill your calling, your life of purpose, to find true and lasting identity, it will come at a price."

He walked back behind the pulpit and stood for a long moment in silence. When he spoke again, his voice was soft and gentle.

"Building on a firm foundation isn't as simple as it sounds. We learn that Jesus set up an inside, outside, an upside down Kingdom where the first was last, and the last was first. To live a life beyond where you are now will require you to die to yourself, to eliminate all the Enemy's access points in your life, and to surrender to Jesus so that he can be Lord over every part of your human experience."

Eli felt an emotion he did not know he'd had welling up inside of him. Something deep within his heart was answering Daniel's call. He had not told his brother about his feelings, the loss and confusion and emptiness he yearned to escape, and yet it was as though every word had been fashioned for his own heart.

He wondered if it was even possible, or if this was the ideological preaching of a man who didn't know any better. Usually, he would have dismissed the sermon as just that. Still, he felt a hunger for more that he could not escape and realized that if it was even a little possible that there was hope for adventure and excitement again, he wanted to know what that hope was.

Daniel began talking about another man from the Old Testament, a man Eli had never heard of before, who had worked for King David as a mighty man of God. He talked about this man and others for some time, and though Eli didn't understand the history behind the stories, he gleaned that his brother was trying to emphasize the role fight and adventure played in the heart of God.

Eli wasn't sure how to accept this. Religion had always been a polite observance for him, a way to remain right on the outside, but now Daniel was saying that there was a place for Eli's wild side in the scheme of the Maker he hardly knew, there was a place for adventure and a life of purpose. The only adventure he'd ever known had come from his time in the service, and his connection to Charlie and Jiu-jitsu...that sort of adventure hadn't been enough for Charlie.

The thought caused Eli to draw a quick, sharp breath. He realized with a jolt that life "not being enough" was what terrified him the most--it had not been enough for Charlie, and so how could it be enough for him?

Eli stood up along with Sarah but didn't leave immediately as he usually did when the sermon ended. Instead, he endured a few casual inquiries about his life and work and then pulled Daniel aside at the first opportunity.

***

"That was interesting," he said, nodding towards the front of the church. "What you said up there today."

Daniel smiled. "I hope so. It's been on my heart all week."

"But I don't understand," Eli went on, talking in a low voice. "If I wanted to live that sort of life that you talk about--a life of purpose and adventure, how would I do that? You say to stay anchored upon the rock, but I don't know what that looks like in my day-to-day life."

Daniel smiled sheepishly. "I really should have been clearer about that," he said. "It's no good to have a pastor who inspires you but fails to give direct instruction. Remember, when I talked about eliminating all the access points, the Enemy might have to undermine you?"

Eli nodded, frowning. That had not been the part of the sermon that had seemed of primary interest to him, and so he had not listened to it carefully. "I'm not sure how to do that."

"Well, are there places in your life where you feel God is not allowed to reign freely? Places where you are indulging in things that are not of Him?"

Eli felt suddenly uncomfortable. He was in a church, after all, surrounded by the self-proclaimed body of Christ. He thought of the things he had looked at on his computer the week before, the words he had spoken to Sarah in anger, the bitterness that seemed always lodged inside of him. He cleared his throat.

"This isn't the place," he said.

Daniel looked around him. "Do you mean because you're thinking of sins in your life? Because trust me, the place to find sinners is in a church. These people struggle with pornography, anger, violence, gossip, and more."

Eli winced. "Then you're telling me to get rid of those things and then just to wait for this grand adventure to arrive?"

"I'm telling you that when Jesus is really and truly Lord over your life--not just in word but in every aspect--you will find yourself with daily opportunities to live with purpose. Which is a Kingdom-driven life." Daniel put his hand out, and, for the first time in a long time, Eli didn't pull away from his touch. "I'm glad you came today, my brother," he said. "Perhaps we could explore this life of adventure and purpose together. I suspect it will challenge us in ways we can only imagine. You up for it?"

Eli looked over at Sarah. She was talking to a group of women in the corner, her face turned away from his. He remembered the passion he had felt for her when they were first married. That excitement, like all excitement, had faded into the black numbness that grew inside him. He wanted that thrill back again. He wanted to feel excited about life again. Then he thought of Charlie, and the chill returned.

"It's worth a try," he said.

Daniel smiled. "Why don't you start by coming to lunch with a few of the elders and I tomorrow afternoon? We meet regularly and would love for you to join. You can pick their brain about this stuff too."

Everything in Eli wanted to run the other direction, but he had promised to try.

"I'll see you then," he agreed reluctantly.

***

After Eli walked out of the church, Daniel turned to John, standing with Eric in the aisle nearby. The two men talked in low tones about something Eric had seen the week before at work, but when they saw Eli leave, they halted their conversation and looked up with interest.

"I've never seen him hang around before," Eric said with a dry smile.

Daniel put a hand to his forehead and gave a little laugh. "We have a God who answers prayers, gentlemen."

"What did he want?" John asked, coming to stand near Daniel.

He had been Daniel's mentor for years, a force of wisdom and support in his life. These three men had been praying for Eli since they'd known each other, coming before the Father, again and again, to ask for freedom and healing in the life of Daniel's brother.

It began as a way to support Daniel, praying for his older brother while Eli was overseas. Still, over the years, the call had changed into something more personal. Daniel saw that Eli had become more than a mission opportunity for John and Eric; he was like an adopted son. Daniel saw these men broken in prayer over Eli and knew that they were entirely devoted to the hope of his salvation and freedom.

"He had questions about the service." Daniel shook his head in wonder. "I don't know...it's like something has clicked in him. "He turned to Eric with a shrug. "Did he reach out to you or anything?"

Eric shook his head. "No," he laughed. "Other than that awkward diner meeting a few years ago, we've hardly talked. I wish he would because I connected with Big O down at the facility, and he says he'd be happy to work with Eli. He says Eli sounds a lot like him--they're both fighters, did you know that? --and he would love to meet."

Daniel sighed. "I keep thinking that if Eli could just be discipled by Big O, it would be a game-changer for him. He only has one example of real manhood that he respects, and that's the men at his gym. He needs someone like Big O that is physically impressive, mentally strong, but also given over to the heart of the Father."

John nodded. "This is nearing the anniversary of Charlie's death, isn't it?"

Daniel frowned. "A few months yet, if I remember correctly. He never talks about it."

"If we try to push him at Big O, he'll see it coming a mile away," Eric said crisply. He seemed to understand Eli better than either of the other two. He had hard edges himself that had been carved away by Jesus and understood Eli's reticence. "He doesn't think he needs any help right now."

"Maybe before," Daniel mused. "But after hearing him talk today, I'm not so sure."

John reached forward, putting a hand on Daniel's arm. "We know what to do," he said, as he always did. "We surrender this back to the Lord, and we surrender Eli to the Lord. The Lord is moving in his heart, and he'll make it happen."

Chapter Three

The Fight

The next day, Eli walked down to the cafe on the pier over his lunch break to meet with Daniel. Usually, he spent his breaks at the old ship museum two blocks over--it was musty and familiar and a place of peace where his mind could rest--but he had promised Daniel that he would try, and this was trying.

The other three were already sitting at a table by the window. Eli recognized John and Eric and felt an occurrence serves. He had avoided Daniel's close friends over the years. They helped move his house, attended his wedding, and sat in the same service alongside him every Sunday, but he managed to keep things casual just as he did at the gym. He didn't need friendships. He didn't need fixing.

"I ordered you a sandwich," Daniel said. "Ours is on the way."

"This is one of those places that specializes in salads and quinoa," Eric said drily, crossing his arms. "I'll bet that sandwich has avocado instead of bacon."

Eli smiled despite himself. If he hadn't had that first awkward meeting with Eric, he might have been tempted to like the guy.

"So, what is it that you gentlemen talk about on these lunches?" Eli asked. "You said they are a regular occurrence?"

"Mostly, we pray," John said with a smile, as though that was the most natural lunch conversation. "But we also talk about our lives."

"So that we can pray about them," Daniel added with a laugh.

"Fascinating stuff," Eli said, looking at his watch.

"Actually," Eric began, clearing his throat. "I thought we could share our Bible plan with you." He flipped out his phone and scrolled to an app. "We're using this one and leaving comments throughout the day--it's a discipleship thing and makes the daily reading a little more approachable."

Eli raised his eyebrows, pulling out his phone to download the app. "I could do that."

John laughed. "Of course, some of us just read it in our Bible and have Eric text us the reference every morning. I can't abide the Word marching across my screen in Times New Roman."

"Also," Daniel added, "You talked about getting more involved in ministry, and I thought you might like to know what options were open to you. I think discipleship would be wise."

Eli took a drink from his water to mask his discomfort.

Discipleship? Like, you guys walk me through the things that are difficult in my life?"

"Sure," Daniel answered slowly. "But I'm wondering if it might be better to connect you with someone who knew a little more about what you're going through."

"I have a friend," Eric interjected gruffly. "Name's Big O. He works down at Kingdom for Warriors Ministries, and he has been asking to meet you."

Eli saw through the whole thing at once. It was like *deja-vu*, sitting here with Daniel again, having his brother set him up with another person to fix his brain, dispel his PTSD, and bond with him over all the people he'd killed. It had been two years, but it was moments like this when he realized how little had changed since he'd left the service.

He pushed his chair back. "You know," he said with a quick smile. "I really appreciate all this help. I do. But my break's pretty short today. Why don't you text me this Big Guy's number, and I'll make sure to reach out."

"You're leaving already?" John asked gently. "Don't you want to wait for your food?"

"I packed something," Eli lied. He had to get out of that cafe. The walls felt as though they were closing in on him, and all the men staring back at him with their good intentions overwhelmed him. "I'll eat in the office."

He hurried outside again and followed the path he usually took down the pier to the ship museum. It wasn't until he was inside with his back against the wall that the rushing sound stopped in his ears. That was the irony of it all: he knew these men wanted to help him deal with his PTSD and trauma, and yet it was the very possibility of facing his monsters that brought them back to him again.

He took a deep breath and looked around. It was quiet because no one ever stepped inside for more than a few minutes. Tourists in the summertime would walk in to catch some air conditioning and then out again when they saw only a single room lined with paintings and artifacts from the 18th-century that could be seen in any *Pirates of the Caribbean* movie.

Eli knew the curator, a man, several generations his senior who came five days out of the week to open the doors and then sat outside on the dock fishing and reading at intervals. He liked the man because he was quiet, didn't force conversation, and at times made Eli feel he had a grandfather to speak to.

Eli looked across at a painting of a whaling crew out in rowboats. Only the great tail of the whale could be seen disappearing into tumultuous greywater. Everything in the picture boded ill for the seamen in the vessel. The clouds were dark, the beast enormous, and the boat looked to be on the verge of tipping over into the sea. Eli liked it.

The curator tottered in the room, a book tucked under one arm, and began his daily dusting off the place. He walked about with a tattered white cloth, likely torn from a t-shirt or some such rag, and gently dusted each piece of the little museum as though it was a well-loved child.

Eli sat up with interest in the words he saw on the curator's book's spine. *Warrior of Old,* it read. He waited until the man was near and cleared his throat to get his attention.

"That book," he said. "What is it that you are reading?"

The man looked down at the book for a long moment and then pulled it out and turned it over in his hands.

"It was my father's," he said quietly. "And before that, it was his father's."

"Is it any good?" Eli asked.

"Oh, yes, it is. Very good." the curator smiled. "Some might say it's the greatest story ever told, next to the Bible, of course."

Eli had not known the man was a believer and felt suddenly uncomfortable.

The old man waited a moment and then held the book out to Eli. Eli hesitated a moment and then took it. He felt strangely drawn to it. He was not an avid reader like Sarah, he had never cared for books, and yet he felt the same way he'd felt at church the day before, as though he was poised on the edge of something new and exciting.

The pages were old and weathered. They had been read again and again. The book itself had an old story's language, a retelling, perhaps, of an ancient myth. Eli's rhythm was unfamiliar, but he looked past the words to the tintype pictures printed every few pages. A knight walked through a wilderness, climbed a mountain, stood by a quiet stream, then, there were ominous figures in the woods, and, at the center of the book, a castle nestled into the mountain range.

Inside the castle, an older man and white-haired, with a staff in one hand and a long medieval tunic. Eli peered at that man for a very long time. Underneath the tintype were the typewriter words: "Warrior of Old."

"It changed my life and opened my eyes."

He jumped at the sound of the curator's voice so near at hand. He hadn't realized that the man was still there, much less leaning over his shoulder as he was now, peering down on him. He cleared his throat.

"What's it about?"

The man did not answer.

Eli frowned at the picture of this Old Warrior again. "This castle seems significant, but I cannot read the inscription over the door." The letters looked Celtic and foreign.

The curator nodded. "Yes," he said, offering no further explanation.

Eli laughed because he didn't know what else to say and handed the book back. "Thanks for your insight," he said with more teasing than sarcasm. He sat in silence for a few moments and then walked back out into the brilliant sunlight of the afternoon.

Daniel had left a message on his phone during the break: *Odd lunch today...talk later?* Eli flipped open the app he'd downloaded. He clicked on the date and saw that the prescribed reading began deep in the book of Leviticus. As he walked along the sidewalk, Eli tried to take it in.

You shall be holy, for I, the Lord Your God, am holy. Off to a grace-filled start, it seemed. He read on, his eyes glazing over. *When you offer a sacrifice of peace offerings to the Lord, you shall offer it so that you might be accepted...*This seemed like the opposite of an adventure. He clicked the screen to black and put the phone back in his pocket.

***

He tried again after dinner that night, but Leviticus was still dense, and his heart wasn't in it. While he scrolled, a message dropped onto his screen: *Friday night, weigh-ins, 10 pm, The Galaxy.*

He felt a surge of excitement but thought of Daniel and put the phone away. He knew that Daniel would disapprove of the fight, and to assuage his guilt, he put the whole matter out of his mind, as though one part of him could serve God while the fighter in him could find an outlet elsewhere.

He walked upstairs and saw that Sarah had fallen asleep on top of the covers, the light still on, a book opens in her hands. He took the book away and pulled a blanket up over her before sitting down on the other side of the bed.

He thought about the Warrior again in the old castle, the long white hair and the set brow for some unknowable reason. He understood now, in retrospect, why the man had seemed so intriguing to him. It was as though the drawing on the page was challenging him to step up to some task.

He sighed and laid down, closing his eyes. It was only a few minutes before he slept, and the nightmares came again, as they always did.

***

By Saturday night, the gnawing feeling of guilt in Eli's chest was utterly overshadowed by the old, familiar panic there. Whatever the cost, the fight loomed in his head as the only way to reclaim even a momentary peace. He made an excuse and went to the weigh-in the night before, going through the spectacle of building anticipation and facing off against Draxler as though there was someone else in his body.

The night of the fight, he told Sarah he had a late night at the gym, the lie joining a long list of lies he'd been telling lately. He wondered if he would eventually grow numb to the look of disappointment and confusion on her face; he asked if he wanted to.

He put away his phone when he reached The Galaxy Hotel. Daniel had been messaging him all day, encouraging him and offering discipleship promptings. It was distracting. There would be time enough to pick up Daniel's holy fight another day. For now, Eli needed to take the feeling of overwhelming emptiness and fill it with something, anything, or he felt he would explode.

By the time he walked into the side entrance the owner had told him about, he had pushed aside all thoughts of Sarah and Daniel, even Charlie. He settled into the blank slate again, thinking only of the fight.

He was shuttled into a room off the side of the ballroom, a much darker room with only a few fighters waiting against the walls, a few warming up in the corner with their coaches, and managers walking along between them advising in low tones.

Eli dropped his bag in the corner, pulled out a jump rope, and got to work. When he felt warm, he moved to slower stretches, preparing for the throws and hits he was accustomed to making. He wasn't intimidated by the more experienced fighters in the room--he didn't even look at them. His mind was on the ring and the relief he knew it would bring.

Eli's coach and Dre from the gym approached him with quick smiles.

"Ready?" asked Coach.

"Let's tape you up. You're on deck," said Dre.

Once taped, Eli and Dre continued Eli's warm-ups by doing light pummeling with him. Then the promoter showed up.

"It's time. We are about to announce to you," he said crisply.

Eli heard his walkout track, *Bodies,* and started into the mass people. The roar of the crowd set the hair on his arm on edge. He came out with his entourage in a single line, Coach in front, Eli with his head down, his hands on Coach's shoulders, towel over his eyes, Dre as his training partner behind. The ballroom looked different from when he first walked in--full and dark, with bright lights on the cage in the center of the room. He had heard about this moment when even the most aggressive fighters have a few moments without adrenaline to consider the terror of the moment sanely before them. He felt a little sick but pushed the fear away as he approached the fight doctor to go through last-minute checks.

Once cleared, Eli climbed the stairs into the caged octagon.

Across the enclosure, there waited a tall, sturdy man with

muscles like cables. *Draxler.* Eli studied him carefully.

The ref called for the fighters in the center of the ring to go over the rules. Draxler looked through Eli rather than directly at him, as though he knew this new fighter was just a small bump on the way to his life in the pros. Eli took a deep breath. The ref then sent the fighters to their respective sides, and the door to the cage was closed.

Eli heard Dre yelling as if from a great distance. "Hands up, tuck your chin, circle right off the line, and be patient."

Eli shrugged the advice away. It was no use cluttering his mind with unimportant facts. He would take the fight to the mat before Draxler had a chance at his face. Eli was king of the world he had chosen, the world of grappling, and any advice to the contrary was only distracting--not useful.

Eli bounced, shifting his weight from left to right, waiting for the bell. The nerves he felt began to fade. The adrenaline was back, the feeling that he could breathe again--that the time bomb could finally explode.

When the bell rang, Eli lunged forward for a single leg. For a moment, everything seemed suspended in time--the emptiness lessened ever so slightly, the adrenaline surged forward and disguised his pain for a blissful second, and then he felt a crack of contact, a left uppercut he had never even seen coming.

His world went black.

"HOPE"

Chapter Four

The Warrior of Old

It was dark and cold.

Eli opened his eyes and looked up, fully expecting to find himself in a back room at the hotel, perhaps in a hospital bed, but he was in neither. The ground beneath him was hard and rocky, there were tall shapes all around him, and the sky overhead was filled with stars. He scrambled to his feet, reaching for his head. There was no wound from the fight, and he didn't feel sore. However, if you could even call it apparel, the clothes he had on were made of what felt like worn sandpaper; the best guess would be burlap, old, rotten, tattered irritant with a stench of death. As his eyes adjusted to the light of the night sky, the large shadows around him were those of trees and more trees. He was in desolate woods.

"Hello?" he ventured quietly, immediately regretting his words. His voice, alone and unanswered, was worse than the silence. *Where am I?* He saw a path ahead of him through the woods, thin and almost entirely overgrown. Everything felt strange, dream-like. He looked down and saw something in his hand, weathered and beaten. He opened it and caught by the light of the moon a familiar face. It was a page torn out of the book the curator had been reading, the page with the old warrior on one side and the castle's map on the back.

He turned it over in confusion. He hadn't taken it, not that he remembered. Who had torn it out of the book, and why did Eli now have it?

Suddenly, he heard something moving in the bushes behind him. It was a distinct sound, not entirely animal, but not entirely human either. The scraping and the panting filled him with a fear he had not known in many years. Once, lying out in a sniper hideout for hours, he had felt that fear when the Enemy came to stand only a few feet away from his position. Now, all thoughts of calm fled. He was in a strange place, perhaps dumped there by the fight organizers, he had this odd piece of paper in one hand, and the distinct feeling that the source of that sound in the woods was hunting him.

He started running and heard the sound intensify behind him, as though the creature sprang forward like a cat. He could taste the terror on his tongue. He rounded the corner in the wood and stopped suddenly in shock. Ahead of him, a small break in the trees framed a mountain range in the distance. He didn't even try to comprehend why such tall mountains would be near his home, for at that moment, he saw something that was undeniably foreign to the pier and his neighborhood and the little church his brother pastored. On the mountain top, glistening in the moonlight, was a castle. No, he corrected himself. This wasn't just any castle; it was *the* castle: the one in the drawing that lay in his palm. He turned the page over and looked from it to the castle on the mountain.

"It can't be," he breathed.

He heard the sound in the bushes again and began to run towards the castle. His mind knew that it wasn't possible, that he couldn't have suddenly appeared in a strange land so far from home, and yet his body knew how to survive, and even as he fought against this new reality, he found his legs rushing on along the path, his brain trying to manufacture an escape.

He cleared the woods, at last, his heart pounding in his ears. There was a path leading up to the castle's gate, not long but steep and rocky. He started the climb, urgency clawing at his heart. He felt as though the answer to this meaningless flight through the woods lay in the castle above.

Once, as he scrambled up the rock face, he looked down. A shadow moved below him, farther back than he feared but still too close for comfort. It looked like a man--cloaked in darkness--but moved too quickly to be human. It seemed like an animal, sharp and quick along the rocks. Eli turned forward again and scrambled up without looking back.

At the top of the rock, he stopped. There was a wide, open place in front of the gate, but no one was on the wall.

"Help!" he called, his voice echoing down the mountain. He heard the scraping again below him and knew his plea was fueling the creature frenzy. "I beg entry!"

There was no answer, but he saw something he had missed before. Words engraved along with the castle's outer gates, written in a language Eli did not know but could read, nonetheless. He walked up to the gates and read aloud.

"Enter His gates with thanksgiving and his courts with praise, give thanks to him and praise his name." He had heard that before. He had even sung it as a child in Sunday school. It seemed nauseating and cliché. He rolled his eyes, nearly forgetting for the moment the danger just behind him. "Am I dreaming?" he called out to the gate. "I can just wake up from this, you know."

He heard a stone drop behind him. The creature was close. "Is it a riddle?" he called out again.

The gates were silent, but in the shadows of the entry, something moved. Eli leaped back, fearful of some other dark and hooded thing, but saw that it was only a man, an old man with long white hair. He was sitting down as though all was well with the world, as though there were not a vicious creature only a few minutes away from attacking him. He had a staff across his lap and only just opened his eyes when Eli jumped away.

"It is not a riddle," the man said. "A riddle needs to be unraveled. These words are unambiguous. They are a direction."

"What, am I to give thanks?" Eli couldn't help laughing wryly. "No one will believe this when I wake up."

"You are not asleep," the man said simply. "And you do not have much time." There was something about the calm in his voice that was more terrifying than Eli's urgency.

"What is that thing behind me?" Eli asked.

"He is the Dark One, and you have brought him to my gates," the man said. "He will not rest until you are his."

"The Dark One." Eli tasted Fear again at the name. It had power, just as the castle's sight had a power, but this was an uglier feeling.

"You are getting distracted," the Warrior of Old said. "Fear is not your friend in this, but I can help you. The gates will open if you offer up praise to the King of the castle."

"Are you not the King?"

"I am a keeper, of sorts," the man said, not answering the question. "But we should not be talking about my history at present. Your future and your past are what dangles over the pit. If I were you, I would offer up thanksgiving--and I would do it now."

"I have nothing to be grateful for," Eli said stiffly. He thought suddenly of the moment in the church the week before when he had closed his eyes during worship and let his mind drift away. The more honest answer came to him suddenly as he looked at the quiet eyes of the Warrior of Old sitting before him. "I don't know how to offer thanksgiving."

The man stood and walked over to him, his movements still slow and unapologetic. He had white hair and the face of an old man, but Eli could see at once that he was strong and sure of himself. "You do not seem like the kind of man comfortable bending a knee," the Warrior of Old said. "But do not fear. It takes many years to learn the strength of humility, and I would not expect you to know how much can be gained by laying down yourself this early in your journey. The smallest movement of your heart towards gratitude will suffice."

Eli closed his eyes, and this time his mind was not blank. He thought fleetingly of his frustrations with work and life, of how much he missed his days overseas, of the explosions that still rang out in his memory after dark, and then he thought of Sarah. She filled his mind for a brief moment, and then a picture of Daniel followed. It was momentary, but Eli's lips moved gently: "Thank you."

And the doors opened.

He heard the scraping and panting behind him again and lunged through the gates. The doors clattered closed behind him, and he turned around to see the Warrior of Old drop a heavy bar into place. Eli stood for a moment, catching his breath, and then looked around. They were not in the castle, after all, but in an outer court of sorts. It was still utterly deserted, but there were weapons along the walls, medieval but not crude. They seemed more elegant than anything Eli had ever used in the desert. They beckoned him. He felt the Warrior of Old's hand on his arm and saw that the old man's eyes had caught the direction of his gaze.

"Not yet," the man said. "Tonight, we make camp."

"Camp?" Eli shook his head. "I don't understand. None of this can be real. Is it some sort of dream? Are you trying to teach me something? If so, what is the need for setting up camp? Didn't I pass the test of gratitude?"

"I find that the line between what is real and what is in mind is far more fluid than people think," the Warrior of Old said quietly, pulling a long strip of leather out of a roll on his back and laying it out on the ground. "You speak as though the gate was the end of something, but it is only the beginning. You have passed no test. You have only entered a place where strength and wisdom have the possibility of coming. Nothing is guaranteed, and where we go next, we will need our rest."

Eli took a step forward, with a muddled look on his face. "What? I don't understand. I am so confused. Look, I just want to get out of here and go home. I don't know what that thing is out there, and now you are saying we are going somewhere?"

"Your journey home requires surrender to the path before you. The choice is yours; however, life and death are in the balance.", explained the Warrior of Old.

Eli was at a loss. The Warrior of Old's words cut to Eli's core. All he could do is attempt to find some sort of answer in the man's eyes. A clue, anything that could explain his predicament. All he could produce was a feeling of loss, for the situation he found himself in was more than he could handle.

"I will be with you, do not worry. All will be explained." the Warrior of Old answered.

He leaned over and began to assemble a fire. He worked slowly and carefully, seemingly oblivious to the sounds that still came from the gate outside. The noise intensified with every passing moment, and there were faint shrieks now, along with the sound of claws running along with the wood. All this the old man quietly ignored, his eyes on his task.

"Will they be able to break through?" Eli asked, a shiver running down his spine.

The Warrior of Old looked up at him with wide, calm eyes. "Would you like some food?" he asked. He pulled out a loaf of bread and a clay jar of something that smelled like meat. He set these, along with cups and a few pieces of fruit, on the leather cloth, and then patted the space beside him as though inviting Eli to partake.

Eli resisted the urge to put his hands over his ears to keep out the sound of the Enemy just outside. "I don't know how you can be so calm," he said desperately, "but shouldn't we move inside? I think I can stand a few more minutes without food if you will only allow me to get away from the sound of my enemy."

The Warrior turned and looked at the door for a moment and then resumed laying out the meal. "I have told you that you are safe," he said quietly. "Why are you still preoccupied with your enemy when I have set the table before you in peace and comfort?"

"I can hear him." The sounds intensified, and Eli was forced to amend his statement. "I can hear *them*. It sounds as though there are more things out there now."

"It always sounds like that if you focus on the thing you fear," the Warrior of Old said quietly. "Remember, fear is not your friend anymore."

"Fear has never been my friend," Eli said sharply, forgetting for a moment the screeching all around him. "I am a fighter and a soldier. I learned to put away my Fear long ago. I am only thinking about my survival."

"You will not truly put away your fear until you understand who you are," the man said. He held out the loaf of bread to Eli, his face still placid and calm. "If you knew your identity, you would not think of yourself so easily forgotten. You would know that the Enemy outside the gate has no real power over your life."

Eli didn't fully understand what the man was saying, but he saw a strange tenderness in his eyes and a warmth in his smile. He thought suddenly, inexplicably, of a father, and for a moment he felt like a son, which is a feeling foreign to him. When people asked about identity, the answer almost always included an explanation of family and history. His father was a question mark, nothing more--evidence that in the end, he would be forgotten by those who were supposed to care for him the most.

"If I eat this," he said, taking the loaf of bread, "will you stay here with me?"

"I will stay here with you, even with the scent of foul garments." The Warrior of Old said, attempting to lighten Eli's mood.

Yet to no avail, Eli felt a stirring of despair welling up inside, an aching as if from unshed tears in his eyes. It had been a long time since he had cried, and he wasn't about to begin now. Still, he took the bread and ate. Unforeseen anguish turned to repressed anger; Eli stared into the fire. The Enemy was still clamoring at the gate, the air still full of eerie sounds.

His world was just turned upside down. In his confusion of where he was at and frustration that he had no other choice but to stay the night with this odd man, in this random place with a terrifying force outside the gates that made this experience more real than the fight which seemed like moments before. Eli resolved to surrender to the perceived circumstances and planned to figure everything out in the morning.

"Perhaps it's just a bad dream." He attempted to reassure himself. *But if it was, why is my skin crawling, literally and figuratively?* His thoughts drifted to Sarah as a single tear rolled down his cheek. *Where am I at; what have I done?*

Chapter Five

The Corridor of Champions

Eli did not remember falling asleep, but he awoke and realized that he had been resting for some time. He was still in the courtyard, and the Warrior of Old was sitting beside him, cross-legged, eyes alert. Eli realized the Warrior of Old had been watching over him, and the thought touched his heart. He scrambled to his feet and listened for the screeching he had heard the night before. The rattle was gone, and in its place, there was an eerie silence.

"Are they gone--is it gone?" he asked breathlessly.

The Warrior of Old shook his head. "The Dark One is only waiting, not gone," he said.

Eli shivered. "You are not very reassuring."

"It is not for me to reassure," the man said, standing and gathering his robes about himself again. "It is for me to make certain that you face the challenges ahead. It is time for us to proceed into the castle. You must make your way through the Three Chambers to the innermost place. There you will find what you need to face the Enemy of your soul."

Eli blinked in astonishment. "I thought the castle was a place for me to hide," he said quietly. "I thought it was a refuge from whatever is crouching outside the gate. Are you telling me that the Enemy will be inside as much as he is out here?"

The Warrior gave a quick laugh and began packing up the provisions he had lain out the night before. "You have never turned away from a challenge before. Why would you start now?"

Eli frowned. "Have we met before this? I do not remember if we have."

The man's only answer was to shoulder the provisions and lead Eli along the outer edge of the courtyard, past the wall of strange weapons, to a great door that Eli had not noticed the night before. He thought it was made of gold initially, but he saw that the gate was merely smooth wood reflecting the golden light of morning when he neared it. There was no riddle above this gate. It opened without even being touched, simply gliding aside when the Warrior of Old held out his hand to it.

"You first," the Warrior of Old said, raising his eyebrow.

Eli hesitated. "You would not have brought me all this way to feed me to a horrible beast, would you?"

"If a son asks his father for bread, will he receive a stone?" the man answered cryptically.

Eli laughed wryly. "You didn't know my father."

He stepped inside. He had expected to encounter the First Chamber the Warrior of Old spoke of, but instead, he came into what appeared to be a long, dark corridor. It was so dark that he could not see the end, but as he stepped forward, a torch flared to light on one side, illuminating a painting hung upon the wall. Eli was not an artistic man, but he felt inexplicably drawn to the painting. He peered at it and pulled back in astonishment.

At first, he thought the flickering of torchlight caused the mirage he was seeing, but upon closer inspection, he realized that the painting before him was alive. It moved and danced, showing an ancient scene. He watched the image, transfixed.

There was a great silver body of water, and a host of people gathered in front of it. They were moving about, splotches of paint come to life, and when he listened closely, Eli heard the sounds of screams coming from the painting. Behind the people, he saw a vicious army riding towards them, brandishing weapons. He had seen the aftermath of genocide during his time overseas, and he knew well what was in store for these people. He wanted to scream at them to fight, but then he saw the inscription beneath the painting. *You need only be standstill.*

He turned to the Warrior of Old standing beside him. "What is this?" he cried. "Why are they not fighting?"

"Watch," was the man's only reply.

Eli saw a sudden flash upon the page and the great silver sea peeled back as though a hand was ripping it in two. There was a tiny strip of brown open now for the people to walk, and they began running through it. Eli knew the story from when he was a child and turned to the man behind him.

"Is it the Exodus?" he asked.

"This is the first monument in the Corridor of Champions," the Warrior of Old answered. "You must walk through this corridor and examine each monument with care. Most of the monuments examine warriors' lives who triumphed over great evil. The corridor displays the monumental moments of triumph through the eyes of the King."

"Triumph?" Eli responded halfway, listening to the Warrior of Old, "It only shows escape. They ran like cowards."

"You are looking at the surface," the man chided him gently. "Not all war is visible to the eye. The King told these people that the Lord would fight for them, that they needed only to stand still and watch his wonders. Sometimes it is harder to stand than it is to fight."

Eli turned and looked at the man, his eyes narrowed. "You speak of war as though it had a place in the Lord's plan. I know this story, and many like it, from my brother's church. He speaks of peace and love. Warriors like me have no place in a peaceful world."

"On the contrary," the Warrior of Old said. His voice was deep and robust, and he seemed almost to grow before Eli's eyes. "There is a war raging, and though it is unseen, you can be certain it is real. You know that evil exists in the world, do you not?"

Eli thought of all the things that he had seen. He nodded bitterly.

"The Dark One is not just an idea. He is an active force, opposing the King's dominion at every opportune moment. He comes not just in violence but in the undercurrent of confusion and doubt that afflicts people throughout their lives. The King is looking for those strong enough to stand up and fight the Dark One.

However, not all battles are won through the blood of man." The Warrior of Old directed his gaze back to the painting. "Sometimes, they are won through faith."

"I don't understand," Eli said.

"Walk on," the man nodded ahead.

Eli stepped forward, and as he did, another torch sprang to life beside him, and another painting became visible. This painting showed two figures locked in a wrestling match. Eli felt strangely at home, watching them circle along the edge of a rushing river.

"Now this, I understand," he said with a smile. "Who are they?" The inscription read-only: *Not until you bless me.*

"That's Jacob," the Warrior of Old said. "He's wrestling with God."

"God?" Eli exclaimed. "I don't remember this particular story. What kind of man would think about fighting God? He's sure to lose."

"This man didn't, not in the way you're thinking." The Warrior of Old looked at the painting with a tenderness in his eyes. "He held on, even after he had been wounded, and told his opponent that he wouldn't let go unless God blessed him. God did. He gave him a new name, Israel, because he struggled and overcame it. He made him a great nation."

Eli frowned. "That's an odd way to reward a man prideful enough to attack God."

"It wasn't pride that made him do it; it was desire." The Warrior of Old turned sharp eyes on Eli. "Haven't you ever felt angry, confused, hungry for more? Haven't you ever desired something from God so desperately that you wanted to fight Him for it?"

Eli felt as though the Warrior of Old's words were laying him bare. "I wouldn't presume," he said, covering his discomfort with a coarse laugh. "I'd be afraid of getting struck by lightning, you know?"

The man didn't acknowledge his attempt to deflect. He stepped forward and put a hand on Eli's arm. Warmth spread from the hand, a sense of belonging. "God is not like you. He is not offended when we are angry with him, and he is not frightened by our confusion. He likes to wrestle because he sees man's, sincere heart. He likes a man who is willing to fight." The Warrior of Old waved ahead into the inky blackness. "Every painting you see will be a monument to the moment in time when God transformed these men into champions."

Eli walked on. The next painting showed a sturdy man with a long beard standing across from another on a hilltop. Below there were two different landscapes--one lush and green, the other desolate. The bearded man stood quietly with his arms crossed while the other screamed at him in a foreign language and pointed demandingly towards the greening grass beyond.

Then the men parted ways, and the bearded man walked for some time across a desert. Suddenly, there came a rider on the horizon who fell down at the man's feet with his hands clasped together. The inscription on the painting read: *Abraham rescues Lot*. The bearded man, clearly Abraham, suddenly turned and raced back the way that he came, intent upon saving the man he had been arguing with at the beginning. Eli shook his head.

"I don't understand. 'Father Abraham' and all that. I know he was important, but isn't this a Corridor of Champions, warriors? I don't remember Abraham being a fighter."

"Of course, he was," the Warrior of Old said with a smile. "But he chose his battles. He only got involved after Lot had been captured, and then he began to act. Lot had chosen the better of two lands and condemned Abraham, his uncle, to the lesser."

"You say he chose his battles, and then you give me a good reason to believe he chose badly," Eli said. "It's not worth fighting for a selfish man like that."

"All men are selfish," the Warrior of Old said gently, the same tenderness returning to his eyes. "But you have the power to fight against that. Abraham was not a man of war, but he was prepared when war came to him, nonetheless. He didn't fight for himself; he fought because he loved his family and wanted to help Lot. There are many motivations to fight, and brotherly love is one of the strongest."

The painting shifted before their eyes, and Eli found himself looking at the same man, Abraham, but this time he was witnessing a very different scene--one he had heard about before: the Warrior of Old was walking up the hill with his son at his side and a knife in his hand.

"See," Eli said in alarm, "I never understood this One. God asks him to sacrifice Isaac, doesn't he? Isn't that a cruel and strange thing to make a father do?"

The Warrior of Old nodded soberly. "It would seem that way at first glance, but there is more to this story than you have yet witnessed." He stepped forward and gestured to the painting. Eli could see that Abraham's face was twisted with grief. "God promised to prosper Abraham, and Isaac was the way that his people would spread over the Earth. Isaac was the promise. This happens so often: whenever we are in the final stages of our promise, God tests our foundations to discover if the promise will become an idol, or if we are willing to submit even that holy thing back to Him."

"What if God hadn't stopped Abraham from sacrificing his son?" Eli asked.

"But He did. He saw that Abraham was willing to give up even the promise for the sake of obedience and submission to God," the Warrior of Old said. "It is an important step for anyone beginning their life of purpose--you must be willing to sacrifice everything, even the promise of God, so that in the end, people can only point to the Lord as the One who provided the success. It is a crucial step for the complete victory of the Warrior, the surrendering of the promise back to the King's command."

He smiled at the painting as the scene changed, and a ram was revealed as an alternate sacrifice. "This is the moment Abraham received all strength and wisdom, this is the moment he truly became Father Abraham when he was willing to give up his most precious thing in obedience to his Heavenly Father."

They moved on to a torch-lit painting of another man in the desert. The inscription read: For they contended with one another. This painting was different from the others. It didn't show an outright battle, but rather a war of actions and consequences. Eli saw that wells dug in the desert that belonged to the man in the painting, but others came and quarreled with him, claiming that the wells were their own.

"This man is Abraham's son, Isaac," the Warrior of Old explained before Eli had a chance to ask him what was going on. "He had to find a way to settle a political matter that was the difference between life and death for his family. His fight involved a show of power, but it also showed the strength of diplomacy."

They walked by more paintings, and each One, the Warrior of Old, paused and shared quietly with Eli. He told him about how the spoiled prince of Egypt, Moses, left the world that had been laid at his feet in pursuit of truth and ended up leading an entire people out of bondage. He spoke of Joshua, Moses' successor, a young upstart who was nevertheless wise and courageous in battle as the people of Israel came into their promised land.

"This Joshua..." Eli stepped closer and examined the painting with care. "He looks as though he is listening to something."

"He is listening to the words of God," the man at his side said quietly. "He had to go forward where Moses could not go--he had to lead a people who rebelled multiple times against their leader, and even against God. He was only able to do that because he listened to the advice and encouragement of the Lord."

"Sounds like powerful encouragement," Eli said drily. "I wouldn't mind having a little of that myself."

"He said," the Warrior of Old quoted, "'Be strong and courageous, do not be afraid, do not be discouraged, for the

Lord your God will be with you wherever you go.'" He paused and smiled. "It is a frightening thing, assuming leadership in the face of a great and terrifying battle, but it is a key step for any Warrior to be prepared beforehand. The King prepares his warriors with words like these: there is no need for fear when the Lord God is at your side."

They walked on. Although he had not known all their stories, the names were mostly familiar to Eli. Occasionally, they stopped by a painting that was utterly foreign to him. One such showed a man with a staff raised in his hand and fire in his eyes, smashing into pieces altars of stone erected on a mountain top. Eli was drawn to the painting more than he had been to anything thus far. The man in it was relatively young, but there was a fire in his eyes and in his movements that spoke of deep conviction and passion. Eli had felt that same fire simmering in his own heart, but he had pushed it down again and again. Here, it is allowed to burn, and it seemed almost righteous.

"Who is this?" he asked. The inscription read: *Who has done this thing?*

He looked at the Warrior of Old and saw an almost mischievous smile in the man's eyes. "Oh, I like Gideon," the man said. "The place where he lived erected altars to a false god, and one night this young man had enough. He crept out under cover of darkness and destroyed all the altars. The false gods' followers were furious and came against him in full force, but it was no use. He called the people to him and fought a great battle."

Eli stepped forward, peering at the picture. The sound of the altar smashing rang out in the dim corridor. Something moved in Eli's heart.

"I want to do this," he said quietly, not even intending to speak but knowing the truth of what he said, nonetheless. "How do I do this?"

The Warrior's eyes were gentle. "If you want to, you need only find the altars erected in your own heart."

Eli frowned. "You say that these paintings depict moments when God transformed these men into champions, right? They feel like altars in and of themselves. Isn't that hypocritical?"

The Warrior of Old leaned on his staff and surveyed the painting before them. "It is true that men often make altars out of their 'defining moments.' A drug addict gets clean the first time, a woman chooses to keep her illegitimate baby, a man survives a drunk driving accident--they all see these moments as their identity, and that can be an altar in and of itself. Just like any false god, those defining moments will eventually disappoint. Imagine if the drug addict slips back into his old habits, then he's not only losing his health, he's also losing the power of that defining moment upon which he placed such a strong emphasis. He loses the will to try again."

Eli shook his head. "I'm not sure I understand. All those things you talked about are good. Isn't it positive to get clean from drugs, to keep a baby, or to avoid drinking and driving?"

"Certainly," the Warrior said. "You are not to deny the moment happened, but you are to create a monument to where God showed up, not where you escaped by your own might. The moment doesn't define you; God defines you." He waved to the corridor. "These monuments are monuments to the One who stepped in and touched your life. He is the only One deserving of an altar, the only One deserving of worship."

Next came the man Eli had been waiting to hear about the entire journey: David. He knew this name from his brother's sermons. He had heard about the King, who was too much of a Warrior to build the temple. He had always identified with that man. He felt as though the blood on his own hands made it hard to walk into the church, hard to live the hallowed life that everyone else spoke about. But David's painting did not show a Warrior battling with great armies as Eli had expected. It showed a child standing in a great field opposite a giant of a man.

Eli felt disappointed. "David and Goliath?" he asked, turning to the Warrior of Old. "You believe this was his monumental moment? This is a child's tale, a story that didn't even involve great military prowess."

"But it involved great courage," the Warrior of Old said. "This young lad had been anointed already by Samuel--he knew he had a great future, and yet he remained a person of no consequence. His brothers were off fighting in the army, and yet he was still herding sheep. But look at him." He leaned forward, waving to Eli to join him. "Look at his face. Does he look like a sheepherder?"

Eli leaned in and was startled by what he saw. It was almost comical--he could see why the giant man was laughing in the painting--because the young boy seemed utterly ignorant of his diminutive size. His little legs were planted firmly, his fists clenched, and his eyes, though frightened, were steely with resolution. He had the body of a child but the face of a Warrior.

"He has a Warrior's self-image," the Warrior of Old said, as though reading Eli's mind. "He was sent to this fight as a messenger boy carrying provisions, and yet he shows up for battle. The Enemy brought their giant because they were fighting a battle of the mind, trying to scare off Israel's armies. But it didn't work: this little boy had already won the battle of the mind. He saw the giant, but he didn't see the Impossible that quaking soldiers behind him saw. He saw only his God, and his God was stronger than the Enemy before him."

After David's painting came a series of genuinely frightening scenes that took Eli entirely off guard. Great and mighty men with rippling muscles and fierce expressions tackled what looked like impossible odds. In one, he saw a man follow a lion into a pit. There was snow drifting all around, and the terrain was rocky and strange. Eli sucked in his breath when the man ran into the cavernous, gaping hole in the ground, and then gasped in relief when he emerged shortly after that with the carcass of a lion in tow.

The Warrior of Old explained that the various fighters were David's mighty men, some whose primary distinction was to protect their King, others who went on to become leaders in the guard and carry out some of the most challenging missions David had to offer.

They continued to walk along. There were kings and lowly servants, warriors, and peaceful prophets. Eli stopped questioning and just listened as the Warrior of Old told their stories. It was the last painting in the hall where he came up short in surprise at the sight of another mountaintop and another altar. This time, there was not a young man destroying it. Instead, the altar was surrounded by hundreds of men in strange garb, changing and praying to some strange god. Eli looked at the inscription: The Lord, He is God.

Eli watched, transfixed, as a white-haired man walked into the group gathered about the altar. The man's face was white with fury. He planted his feet beside the stone and began to speak in a foreign tongue. Eli listened and found that it was as it had been by the gate outside. Though he did not know the language, he understood what the man was saying.

"I am the only man left who speaks for God," the white-haired man said. "But there are 450 men here who speak for Baal. Bring two bulls for us. Let them choose one bull for themselves and cut it up. Put no fire under it. I will make my own bull ready. We will each call upon our gods, and the god who answers by fire, He is God."

Eli saw the same passion in this man's eyes that he had seen in Gideon's, and he felt as though the man was calling to him. He watched as the other gods' priests made their altar and began bowing and praying before it. Chills ran up Eli's arms as he watched, but no voice from Heaven came. Eli watched in his own time, yet it seemed that an entire day passed in the painting. The false god remained silent. Then the white-haired man prepared the other altar and prayed: "Answer me, oh God of Abraham, Isaac, and Israel so that these people might know that you are God so that they might turn their hearts to you again."

Fire flashed down from Heaven and consumed everything, the altar, the trenches of water about it, and the sacrifice. Eli felt his chest suddenly seized with powerful emotion, and he doubled over, trying desperately to catch his breath. It was as though the fire from the painting had flashed out and was licking at the edges of his altars. He stumbled back and closed his eyes for a long moment. When he opened them again, the painting was still.

"Who was that?" he asked.

"That was your namesake," the Warrior of Old said, stepping forward. "That is the legacy that is engraved on your heart."

"His name was Eli?"

"Your name is not Eli. From now on, you are to be called 'Elijah,' the prophet who spoke the words of the Lord and saw truth come with fire to consume a righteous offering."

Eli shook his head. "I do not understand."

"It is not so unusual for God to change the name of a man when he has shown that man a true purpose at last," the Warrior of Old said with a smile. "We have seen other such stories even today. Think of Jacob, who wrestled with God and then was given the name Israel. There are others--God provides a purpose, strength for battle, and the wisdom to co-rule with him on Earth as we build his Kingdom. It is in His very nature to help us walk in this identity."

Eli looked back at the painting, at the fire consuming the altar, and felt the pressure in his chest again.

"My name is Eli," he said softly, clinging to what he knew--afraid of the other name and the purpose it carried along with it. "I do not know that man, and I could not be like him."

"Why could you not be like him?" the Warrior asked. He seemed to mean the question genuinely, kindly.

Eli shook his head. "He speaks with God as though he knows him. He stands at the edge of the altar and calls down the fire with absolute confidence. I have no such confidence. I don't know that God will come through for me."

"The King is trustworthy."

Eli frowned. "Perhaps He is," he said. "But if I cannot trust anymore, it doesn't matter how trustworthy He is."

"No matter," the Warrior added with a smile, unperturbed. "The King is also patient."

He turned and walked to another door nearby.

"We cannot tarry here," he said. "Keep all these things treasured in your heart, for now, we are stepping into the great Hall of Atonement, and you will need all that you have learned thus far."

Eli stepped after him, anticipation and fear mingled in his heart.

Chapter Six

The Hall of Atonement

The room they stepped into was unlike anything Eli had ever seen. Until this moment, everything in his experience of this strange world had been almost primitive in its ancient simplicity: the woods around the castle, the night spent sleeping in the courtyard, and the dimly lit Corridor of Champions. The hall into which they stepped now showed signs of elegance and grandeur.

The walls were high and straight, and over the stone hung tapestries and strange weapons. The ceiling curved upwards, the beams alternately arching towards the peak and dipping back down again to hold three massive lanterns far overhead. They were not lit, and there were no windows, but a grand hearth at one end of the room kept the room alight with flickering firelight. Eli noticed upon closer inspection that the light from the hearth was brighter and whiter than he had ever imagined fire to be, and it burned so fiercely that he began to suspect it was more of a furnace than a fireplace.

He felt drawn to the flames, yet he was frightened at the same time. It seemed to him that there was something else waiting beyond the fire, as though the furnace was a gateway. Between him and the flames, there was no furniture--only a solitary circle of stones. Eli felt, rather than saw, the circle. He tried to glance at it once or twice but found it difficult to look at. A cold chill crawled up his back at the thought, and he kept his eyes fixed on the flames instead.

"Shall we go forward?" he asked quietly.

"If you want to," the Warrior answered him.

Eli realized that he did want to--more than he'd wanted anything in a long time. The dream-like quality of the experience was fading further and further away, and the adventure before him seemed real, tangible.

He took a step forward without stopping to deliberate, but when he was halfway along in the direction of the circle of stones, he felt a great force pushing against his body. He stumbled backward towards the door and towards the Warrior of Old, trying to catch his breath.

"What was that?" he asked, looking around the room. Nothing else had changed. The circle of stones was the same, the flames in the fireplace flickered on, and the silence was still complete.

His companion said nothing, and so Eli attempted to step forward again. Again, the invisible force pushed him back. It slammed against him with the strength of a prizefighter, and he found that the stronger he fought to move forward, the more he fell behind. When he stopped battling the force, at last, he was closer to the door than when he had begun.

"Why can I not go forward?" he asked the Warrior again, turning in frustration.

"Why do you want to?" the man asked in response, a smile playing on his lips. "You told me earlier you think this is all a dream. Why does it matter if you move forward through the castle or not?"

Eli understood with startling clarity that he would never be satisfied until he had gone the distance of this adventure, whatever the end might bring. He couldn't explain why, but he felt as though the mystery of this strange place held the answer to the ache of longing and loss in his own heart.

"I want to go on." He felt that somehow the adventure ahead was what he had been looking for all these years, even before the military, before the fights. "I'll do whatever it takes."

The Warrior of Old stepped forward, and his face seemed suddenly gentle and sad, as though his heart was filled with compassion for the young man standing before him. "You cannot," he said, "Until you have given your life to the Son of God the Father, Jesus Christ. It is the only way you can complete this journey as you ought."

The words were like cold water on Eli's excitement. He took a step back from the Warrior of Old. "I thought this was a dream-- an adventure. Not a sermon."

"This is certainly an adventure," the Warrior said, "but it is not a dream. It is more like a...a vision if you would."

Eli drew a shallow breath. "You're telling me this is real?"

"I'm telling you that if you want to conquer the darkness in your life and walk in fullness, at last, you are going to have to make a decision here--and that decision must be for Christ."

"The King of this castle?" Eli asked.

"God the Father, and Jesus Christ, His Son. When you see the

Son, you have seen the Father." The Warrior of Old walked forward and put his hand on Eli's arm. The touch felt like fire. "I'm telling you that this is as real as can be--your decision here will affect your heart and your soul, and there is no battlefield more impactful."

Eli took a deep breath. "Daniel will never believe this," he said wryly.

"You underestimate your brother," the Warrior of Old smiled. "He would be more at home here than you know." He stepped aside, folding his hands around his staff. "Now, you must decide--are you ready to give your life over to the Son?"

Eli took his hand forward and felt the quivering power in the room at his fingertips. "I go to church," he said. "I do the right things. Surely Jesus Christ is a part of my story already."

"To be truly saved by a knowledge of Him, you must have a knowledge of your need for Him, and an understanding that you are unable to stand before the Father without receiving the gift of atonement for your sins: the ultimate Gift presented to you through the death, burial, and resurrection of your Lord, you're Savior, Jesus." The Warrior pointed to the circle of stones at the center of the room. "There is a well there. Go to it, and look into it. You will see and understand."

"I cannot walk to it," Eli said. "Something is pushing me back." He also thought that he didn't *want* to walk to it. He felt a cold breeze stirring from what he now knew was a well, and he wished he could move towards the furnace without passing that darkness.

"I will walk with you." At that, the Warrior seized his arm in a mighty grasp and began to lead him over to the stones. With the Warrior at his side, Eli moved through the invisible force in the room without difficulty. He still felt the pressure and the fear, but he also knew that he would not be thrown backward as long as the Warrior of Old was near. At the edge of the well, he stepped away and found he could stand on his own. He put his hands on the stones and leaned over the side to look down into the darkness below.

What he saw shook him to the core. He had no doubt now that this experience was more real than even his life on Earth had been, for there before he was a darkness that he knew better than any other--the darkness of his own heart. He saw the shadows below evoking scenes from his past that he had never said to another soul: things he had done, and, worse, things he had only thought of doing. He wouldn't have been able to tell such things even to himself, and yet here he was with the murderous, lustful, treacherous parts of his own heart climbing up the walls of the well as though to devour him.

Eli fell backward, his hands leaving the edge of the well as though he had been burned. "No," he said, shaking. He felt a cold sweat on his forehead. "Why must I look there? I do not want to see."

The Warrior of Old looked very sad. "It is a devastating thing to know one's own depravity, but you cannot move on until you have realized your need for a Savior. You must look into your own heart."

Eli thought of all the wars, battles, and bravery that made up his past. He had thought himself a solid and courageous man, and yet now he realized that he was more frightened of the contents of his own heart than he was even of the Dark One crouching outside the gate of the castle. He thought fleetingly of turning back and giving himself to the darkness outside rather than dealing with the darkness within, but the eyes of the Warrior of Old held him steady.

"I will try once more." He went back to the well, his fingers touching cold stone again, and steeled himself for what he would see.

This time, the phantom images of his own darkness were quicker and sharper than before. He saw clearly the moments that he had taken pains to forget over the years--the moments when he had been most disgusted with his own thoughts and actions. Suddenly, it was as though the room around him was falling away, and he felt himself slipping down into the well instead of standing atop it. The stones inside were slimy and cold, and though he tried to cling to them, Eli found that the creatures below were pulling him further and further down, one stone at a time. He called out for help, and then, when no answer came, called out for the only name he could remember in this pit of darkness.

Jesus. "Jesus!"

The answer was immediate. There was no more waiting, no more wondering, and no more fighting. There was only a bright, searing light, and a hand, and he was suddenly out of the pit and standing beside it again. He saw the Warrior of Old standing to one side, but it was not the Warrior of Old's hand that had rescued him. It was another, belonging to a figure standing before Eli.

"Are you…"

All the darkness of the well and the creatures within it seemed to vanish as Eli looked at the man before him--a young man, perhaps--or an old one, it was hard to know just as it was hard to know with the Warrior of Old. He had soft, dark skin and deep brown eyes, brown hair to his shoulders, and a white wrapped robe. He looked at Eli as one might look at a brother, with tenderness and delight.

"I AM," the Son of God said. His voice was music and dancing and prayer all in one, the strength and wisdom of the universe in two distinct words.

Eli knew Him immediately, yet his speech evaded him. He could only bow his head and look at his feet. Before him, the man was so beautiful, so pure, so holy, and he had pulled Eli out of thick darkness. He had seen all of Eli's failings, and Eli was filled with shame at the thought.

He felt something cool suddenly at his feet and looked down in surprise to see that water was welling there around his ankles, overflowing from the well. Before, it had seemed as though he was falling into an endless pit, but now the water was pouring over the rim of the stones, spilling down in clear currents to the ground, and washing away everything that Eli had seen in the darkness.

"The water of life," the man said with a gentle smile. "There is no room for anything now, but the overflow." The man spoke again, turning away from the well. "I am walking on," he said gently. "Come, and I will share with you all that you are to be."

Eli found his tongue at last, quavering and thin. "I will, but I have many questions," he said.

"Good," Jesus said, laughing lightly and suddenly like a child. "I have gone into the well of your soul, and I have brought you up out of your heart of stone. Elijah, my brother, my child—come with me."

And at that moment, Elijah fell away. Perhaps he laid down by the well for all eternity, perhaps he went back to the gate-- perhaps he ceased to be entirely. It did not matter to Elijah, the man who had been reborn and was now walking alongside his Savior towards the flames ahead. The Warrior of Old walked with them too, and when they reached the furnace, he pointed to it gently.

"Elijah, you must go through the flames to move onwards. The fire will not harm you as long as you are with me. It is meant to burn away all that is rooted in decay. Your filthy clothes are woven by the threads of your sinful nature. Your old self that turned to anger, rage, malice, slander, lies, curses, pride, anger, bitterness, lust, greed, worry, and impatience are the source of the smell of sulfur emanating from the garments of ash you wear. The furnace, my holy fire will cleanse you." Jesus said.

Elijah felt the heat searing against his face and took a step backward. "I want to go on," he said, "but is it wrong that I am frightened to have to walk through those flames on my own?"

The son laughed with the same gentle, delighted joy. There wasn't a shred of sarcasm or judgment in that laugh. Elijah felt Christ's pleasure. "You will not have to walk through the furnace alone," he said. "I will go with you. Let's enter." He held out his hand, and though Elijah could feel the heat still, he could no longer feel the fear. He took hold of his Savior's hand and stepped forward into the fire.

There was a searing white pain at first, and then nothing. He was standing inside the furnace looking about himself at the flickering fire against the walls, feeling a movement of wind against his face and arms and hands, and yet there was no pain at all. He looked down at his own feet and saw the flames parting around his footsteps. He understood that it was a strange miracle that he should be surrounded by such violence and be untouched, but he was even more delighted to feel the fear licking away from him as well.

He saw the eyes of the Son and knew the reason for his confidence. It was a visceral place of cleansing and sanctification--a place to fear--, but there was no room for anything but the Truth of Christ in those flames. Fear would have to wait outside.

Then Jesus said, "Elijah, I have taken away your sin, and I will put fine garments on you. Come with us, my son."

Chapter Seven

The Garment of Christ

Elijah stepped out of the furnace and into the lighted room on the other side, following his two companions. He felt clean, but a strange sort of clean that he never had before experienced, as though all the darkest corners of his heart had been examined and purified. At first, he could think of nothing but that sensation of light, airy cleanliness, but then his eyes adjusted, and he saw that he was at the bottom of a curving staircase leading upwards.

The room at the staircase base was small and simple, but Elijah felt safe and peaceful there. He knew even before the Warrior of Old spoke that he would not be allowed to remain in that room for long, but he closed his eyes and soaked in the peace of the moment. When he opened them, he was startled to find that only the Warrior of Old stood beside him. While his eyes were closed, the Son had disappeared.

He felt the loss at once.

"Where did Christ go?" he asked. "He said he would not leave me."

"He has not left you," the Warrior of Old said with a small smile. "Just because you cannot see him does not mean he has gone."

Elijah felt a grain of fear return. This reminded him too much of his life before the vision--of things that Daniel would teach about from the pulpit. "I don't want to go back to living a life where I profess a faith in Someone I never see or feel or hear," he said, a little desperately.

"You are assuming that you never see him or feel him or hear him," the Warrior of Old said. "But He is not as fickle as that, and his love is not so fragile. You need only tune your heart to listen."

Now, look at the holy garment you are wearing." At that moment, the Warrior of Old placed his hands on Elijah's shoulders. Not noticing the new clothing at first, Elijah marveled as his beautiful garment began to glow, shimmer, pulsate with light as if the rays themselves were alive. The material was unlike anything he had ever felt, thick, impenetrable but silky and light-weight. The fabric appeared to be woven with gold, however as Elijah's eyes focused more on the colors, his eyes began seeing shades of blues, purples, and scarlet yarn, with finely twisted linen intertwined. There were tassels on the corners, with a blue cord on each tassel. Elijah originally thought the smell of incense in the fire turned to be a wonderful fragrance coming for the garment. "It is the fragrance of the cedars in Lebanon." Explained the Warrior of Old, reading the mind of Elijah.

Examining the garment further, Elijah noticed it was without seams. "Is this Jesus' robe? I can't wear this." It was the long, white robe that Christ had worn. He was astonished as he looked upon it and even more astonished it had appeared on him.

"I cannot wear His clothes," Elijah said. "It would be like pretending to be Him."

"It is a good deal more than that," the Warrior said. "It is assuming His identity and laying aside your own. You will find, I think, that such a thing is not so very hard after going through the flames as it would have been before the furnace. You already allowed the goodness of the Son to sear your heart to the core. You have already accepted your new name. Now it is time for you to walk in His steps, clothed in the threads of his righteous character."

"I will lose a part of my identity," he said quietly. It had always been a great fear of his, the loss of who he was. He had taken care to build his own image and reputation in the world of the military, the church, the gym. Eli had been a well-crafted face put on for the world to see and admire, and yet here, Elijah was setting aside all of that and assuming the identity of a different person entirely. The fear returned, but his excitement grew as well. "It will be like a kind of death."

"There is a death that is more like life," the Warrior said. "You have been living for some time as one who is dead in spirit; you wore your sin like the decaying garment that burned away and also your heart. You have hoped and prayed for something to fight for, something to come alive for. Dying to your old self and stepping into the newness of Christ's character will be more of birth than death. The Baptism of Fire.

You must discover the secret to wearing his robe, the Garment of Christ. This is the signification of his deep, unconditional love for you. In this, you derive your confidence and freedom you need to develop; as you grow closer to Jesus. You are never to search for the garment of sin and death. For one can abandon the Garment of Christ and return to the decaying stench of clothing. You no longer have to attempt to fit into society and hope you don't explode in a fit of rage. That way of acting, thinking, and behaving burned away in the fire. Instead, the new garment bestowed to you contains the virtues of Christ in every thread. It is the very source of its splendor. The virtues are the fabric and will penetrate your being; as long as it is worn. Even as I speak, the threads of virtue are penetrating you, Elijah. Allow it to take its course. You will learn more about the secrets of this garment as you progress on your journey. The Garment of Christ will be the symbol of your new identity in Jesus and will serve to guide you. It is the bridegroom's gift to one elevated to a saintly priest. Even now, the change has begun."

As one notices changes in seasons, Elijah began witnessing the changes of mood in his soul.

"Can you tell me more about the change that is happening in me? The virtues?" asked Elijah.

"These seven virtues woven into the Garment of Christ are forgiveness, peace, kindness, humility, love, patience, and praise—all are present and operate in you as you surrender to the One who gave you the garment.

Forgiveness is a virtue that is two-fold. Forgiving others who have wronged you because you were forgiven by the One who saved you; serving to clear the poison of bitterness out of your soul.

Peace is the virtue that creates an atmosphere that establishes the presence of the King. It is strong enough to overcome any stressful feelings that try to overwhelm you, Elijah. When allowing this virtue to work within the Garment of Christ, it will begin to free you of the unnecessary stress the Dark One sends your direction.

Kindness is the virtue that will reset the way you treat all people. Your flesh is calibrated to look to your own for your interests first, then potentially look to the interests of others. This is not how a Kingdom Warrior is to live. Surrender to this virtue; the Garment of Christ will prompt you when people need encouragement, comfort, or help. Kindness is most effective when it is a part of you, acting as part of your nature and not requiring thought to execute. It will expand your observation to take advantage of every opportunity to respond to others who need to hear a kind word or to show them kindness in action. Those that are merciful will also be shown mercy. Understanding this truth will provide you protection.

Humility as a virtue prevents the destructive behavior of pride from operating within you. For pride is the root of all sabotage. Abandon your selfish ambitions, for it only derails you from your Kingdom purpose, the reason you were created. Grace is only given to the humble; Heaven will not partner with the prideful one. Humility exposes the sinful nature creating chaos in your life; it is an opportunity to come to Jesus for help in the mission given. Moreover, humility is firmly rooted in knowing who you are in Jesus, Elijah. It is knowing you came from God the Father, and you are going back to God the Father. You are His. Therefore, receive the fruit of this virtue, which is freedom of worrying about *self,* the by-product of pride.

Love, the greatest of all virtues, and the highest display is compassion in decisions for others. Actions towards your brother should carry this virtue; operating with just a sense of duty falls short of full effectiveness. Elijah, love will reveal the people around you; listen to their testimonies to understand their challenges and then move as the King's wills you to. Love is the catalyst of healing by reversing the damage brought forth by the destruction of sin in people's lives.

The patient is a virtue that allows access to a renewed strength when waiting on the Lord's timing in your life. A good example to illustrate this virtue would be exercise. Just like your muscles grow when you train like a fighter, Elijah. There are many resistances and sometimes tremendous pressure. You will see good results when you allow this virtue to train you. Allow the Garment of Christ to develop patience in you as you make sacrifices to build stronger relationships.

Lastly, Elijah, you may recall what gave you access into this Kingdom's gates?

"Thanksgiving, praise?" Elijah said.

"Yes, that is correct, firmly rooted in the joy of the Lord. Happiness in self-gratification is fleeting—temporary feelings of emotional bliss. However, it is the grateful joy of praising the King for who He is and what He has already done for you, lasting power, no matter how your circumstances change at the moment.

As stated before, more will be revealed to you along the journey. It is not for you to have full understanding only to possess the Garment of Christ and surrender to its teachings." Said the Warrior of Old.

A small door opened, and out of the hideaway, the Warrior

pulled a vial of liquid. He uncorked the vial in his hand, tipping something like oil onto his fingers and then brushing his hands across Elijah's forehead and shoulders.

"You are sealed in the Son," the Warrior of Old said quietly.

Elijah didn't know what that meant, but he felt completeness, a wholeness. "Is this the end of the journey?" he asked. "Surely, there is nothing more to be learned or done after a connection with Christ. Surely this is the highest thing."

"In many ways, it is the highest thing," his companion smiled. "But it is not the end; it is the beginning. Until now, you have only been living a half-life, but now you must face the things of the world with your new perspective and your new weapons." He held out his hand towards the narrow staircase before them. "Climb to the rooms above, and we will put your new garment to the test."

Elijah bit his lip. "Are you leaving me now, too?"

"I will never leave you," the man answered gently.

Together, they stepped onto the winding staircase and began to climb together.

Chapter Eight

The Access Points of the Enemy

In all the personal exploration and overcoming, Elijah had nearly forgotten the Dark One that had first driven him to the castle to hide, but as he climbed higher and higher in the close staircase, he began to remember the darkness he had been fleeing, and he began to wonder about the words his companion had spoken back in the courtyard: about how a time would come to fight the Dark One. He wondered when that time would be and if he would be ready.

When the staircase ended, at last, he found himself in a round room with a conical roof. He was startled because this was the first place in all their wanderings that looked at all familiar to him. The room still had medieval stone, but there was a mat and a boxing ring set up with ropes for sparring in the center. There were benches along the edge, and at the far end of the room, there was a great door over which a sign read: *The First Chamber.*

"It is time to sit and rest," the Warrior counseled him, going to one of the benches and taking a seat.

Elijah walked to the ring, running his hand along the edge of the ropes. The smell of sweat and canvas hung in the air. It was all jarringly familiar, jerking him back to memories from before the adventure in the castle. The Garment of Christ felt heavy.

"I would rather go on," he said frowning. "I have the energy and passion now. I am not afraid of what lies behind that door, and I am eager to learn all I can."

"And you are not too keen to stay here, I imagine," the Warrior of Old said with a look of keen understanding. "But you must not rush on to the next adventure without first determining you have left the way behind well and safely guarded."

Elijah looked around him. "No one has followed us," he said. "You told me that the Dark One would remain at the gate."

"The Dark One is clever."

"But there is only the door behind us and the chamber ahead," Elijah said.

"That is not quite true." The Warrior of Old stood and leaned against his staff, his eyes sober.

At that moment, Elijah became aware of a scratching sound coming from the wall nearest to him. He turned and saw with horror that a stone was sliding away, ever so slowly, and out from behind the stone came a scrawny dark leg. It scrambled out and was followed by seven other legs and a body. It was the largest spider Elijah had ever seen, about the size of a small chair, with sharp beady eyes and a quick scuttling gate. His skin crawled as the creature scrambled over the floor towards him.

He turned frantically towards the Warrior behind him and saw that the man was already holding a sword out to him. The sword was sharp and straight, glistening in the dim light. There were carvings on it that were strange--engravings he could not decipher--and if the situation had been less dire, he would have taken the time to examine it further. Elijah had used many weapons in his life, but he had never wielded one like this. It fit his hand as though it had been made for him. He lunged forward at the first creature, missing at first but then hitting twice with success. The third stroke of the sword slit the creature across the middle, and it fell senseless at his feet.

Elijah felt suddenly ill and stepped back from the dead thing in disgust. "What is it?" he asked. "Why did it come for me?"

Before the Warrior of Old could answer, there was another sound of scuttling, but this time from a different side of the wall. By the time Elijah had turned with his sword at the ready, there were two spiders, just as large and terrifying, crawling out of the wall behind him. They skittered along the floor in his direction, just as the other one had. He swiped at them, hard, and though he was more efficient this time, he had only just killed them when he heard his companion call out, "Behind you!"

He turned and saw that two more stones had opened in the wall. There were at least five spiders now skittering towards him. He leaped into the center of the ring, swiping frantically with the sword. The Warrior of Old began to fight as well, using his staff with great, strong sweeps across the room. At first, Elijah thought they would triumph, but the more spiders he killed, the more seemed to arise from the trapdoors in the room.

There were nine openings now, and though no more stones moved, the spiders skittered out in ever-increasing numbers.

"What should we do?" he cried to the Warrior of Old.

"You have to shut the doors!" the man answered, his voice faint over the sounds of the battle. "You and you alone can shut them, for you were the one that opened them in the first place."

Elijah didn't understand. He had not wanted to open any doors in the hall, he couldn't remember having done anything to bring the spiders, but he had learned enough by now to follow the advice of the Warrior without hesitation. He turned and began fighting his way towards the first of the openings. He heard the Warrior behind him covering his advance, but it took all his effort to keep the creatures at bay as they tried, again and again, to swarm over him.

At the first small stone door, he looked down and saw with a start that there was a word inscribed in the wall, etched as though with a chisel: *Pride.* He pushed hard against it, but it would not move. He turned desperately to the Warrior of Old, who happened to glance his way at the same moment.

"How do I close it?" he asked.

The Warrior swiped hard against a mass of the descending swarm and then called the instruction quickly over the fray. "You know by now that prayer is stronger than striving, Elijah," he said. "If you have left access points open to the Enemy, then repentance is the surest way to close them again."

It felt strange to Elijah to stand beside the mat, the symbol of his ability to take matters into his own fists, and instead choose to pray, but he stopped in the battle for a moment and planted his feet firmly on the ground, calling out in a loud voice to the King of the castle, "I know that my pridefulness keeps me from honoring You," he called. "I repent of what I have done, and what darkness I've let into my life through this sin."

The stone moved, sliding like butter over the wall and dipping back into place. No more spiders came from that opening, but the fight had only begun. Getting to the other doorways was difficult--he had to wade through the creatures that had been let in from his other sinful moments just to address one access point--and even when he reached the doorways, the moments of prayer and repentance were as draining as the physical battle.

Elijah winced to see the things that he had allowed into his life. Some of the doorways he expected, like "Unbelieving Heart," which had prevented his knowledge of God and His ways, and "Prayerlessness," which had hindered God's peace and presence in his life. But there were other access points that he had not known were in his heart. "Victim Mindset" let loose a slew of spiders that were formidable in their attack, and Elijah had to repent of his excuses and lack of responsibility before the stone finally slid back into place.

At every place, before the stone was sealed again, Elijah found himself facing memories of specific moments when the door to darkness had first opened in his heart. Some of those moments were choices he had made, things that he had wanted more than God. Some of those moments were things that had been done to him that he had never addressed or fully healed.

When the room had finally closed again, and all the creatures let loose were dead, Elijah fell to his knees, exhausted.

"I don't understand," he said. "I wear the Garment of Christ. I walked through the furnace, and I was sealed in Him. Why is the journey still so difficult? Did he not go back to these dark moments and take away my shame?"

"He did," the Warrior said gently. "But sanctification and renewing of the mind is a daily process, and uprooting the strongholds of the Enemy can be a violent endeavor. Beware of the ploy of the Dark One's intervention into your life and zealously defend the freedom that Christ has granted you. Repentance to the King is the key for continued freedom from evil sabotage."

Elijah was drained, weary, but full of victory as he stood and leaned on his staff.

The Warrior of Old sat again on the bench, as though all the excitement had not just occurred. "I have watched men for all eternity," he said, tapping his fingers against the edge of his own wooden staff. "They go through conversions as you did in the lower hall, they see the hand of God in their life, and then they begin to wonder why they continue to be in a place of sabotage when in every other way they have understood themselves to be right with God." He smiled kindly. "It is access points like the ones you have identified here that so often pull men back into despair."

"I do not remember inviting these moments into my life," Elijah said quietly.

"Often, the agreements with darkness are more subtle," the man responded. "Sometimes they come by means outside our control, in moments we do not expect. Do you remember the unforgiveness that you identified at the far end of the room?"

"I do." Elijah didn't look in that direction. He knew a particularly large pile of defeated creatures would be lying there.

"Allow me to show you something." The Warrior of Old stood from his seat and walked to the ring in the center of the room. He helped Elijah inside through the ropes and then retrieved a rolled canvas from one of the corners. Elijah had not noticed it before. The Warrior of Old unrolled it, using the ropes of the ring as support.

Elijah saw at once that it was another painting, like the ones he had seen in the Corridor of Champions. The style was the same, but the characters in it were familiar to him--the scene was one that had been imprinted on his heart his entire life. He felt the same urge he had felt when he was in the well before Christ came to rescue him, the urge to look away and save himself the pain of his memories.

He didn't, however. He forced himself to hold steady and stare at the figures on the canvas surface. They moved gently. He saw himself in the kitchen of his childhood home, pretending to draw within the lines of a coloring book while his brother Daniel sat sniffling beside him. He saw his mother, angry, hurt. He heard his father crashing about in the other room and knew that they were all waiting for his anger to subside. He knew what the little boy in the painting hadn't known then--that it was the last time he would ever hear those sounds from his father. The man had left, had chosen the easy way out, and abandoned his family.

Elijah had never said the words aloud, but in his heart, he had resented the God that would allow that to happen even as he sat in the pew at church, went through the motions of his marriage, and spoke with his brother about discipleship.

"Do you remember what you used to say to God?" the Warrior asked quietly. "Because the King remembers."

Elijah hung his head in shame. "I said that if he was really God, he would have helped me. He would have given me a father worth having--he would have protected my family from the abuse and from the abandonment." He felt the heaviness of that moment. "I am ashamed of my anger. I hate that the King can see it."

"That is not what the King remembers." The Warrior of Old had the softness of infinite compassion in his eyes and put a hand on Elijah's arm. This time it did not feel like fire--it felt like hope and comfort. "The King remembers a little boy that was hurting. He is not afraid of your doubting, and he is not angry at your anger. His heart breaks for the boy in the picture. His heart breaks for you."

Elijah felt the tears welling up within him. "It seems scandalous," he said, "that I should be allowed to stand before such holiness and bring my anger and hurt with me."

"He is a scandalous King," the Warrior said, shrugging. "And He is not crushed by your pain."

He rolled up the painting and tucked it into the folds of his cloak. "But you need not carry your hurt any longer. He will hold it for you. He will give it the respect it deserves so that you can walk free of it." He nodded towards the door near at hand. "It is time for us to walk on. Are you ready?"

Elijah nodded and looked down to where the sword had been in his hand, surprised to find his palms empty. He frowned. "The weapon," he asked, "where has it gone?"

"You will need the sword again before long," the Warrior of Old said soberly, "but now is not the time for you to carry it. First, it must be forged rightly in wisdom and might, and only then will you be able to carry it as you ought. Until such a time, you must go on without it."

Elijah turned towards the door to the First Chamber, at last, his heart lighter than it had been before. With the Warrior at his side, he set his hand upon the latch and pushed onwards in the journey that lay ahead.

Chapter Nine

The Chamber of Strength

Elijah entered the First Chamber with caution after the spiders' battle, his eyes watching carefully for enemies. He was shocked by what he saw. Unlike the other rooms in the castle, this one was full of people. They were gathered around something in the center of the room and were dressed in strange and foreign clothes: long robes that fell to the ground, shorter tunics on some, men with beards, and women with their hair caught up in scarves. They all looked as though they were from a different time than the era of the castle. There was not a knight or lady in their midst. They looked as though they had stepped out of one of the paintings in the Corridor of Champions--as though they had stepped out of the Bible.

They were standing in a room that was larger than any Elijah had yet seen, and though the people themselves seemed to have come out of some ancient desert land, the surroundings were still that of a castle. The ceiling was so far overhead that Elijah couldn't fully see it without squinting into the inky blackness. The walls were bare, but the stone was so elegant and smooth that they needed no decoration.

The people were gathered in the center of the room in a wide light made by an enormous lantern that hung down near the ground. There was a portico of sorts erected beneath the lantern, and the crowd was gathered around it. Elijah could not see what they were looking at, but he was distracted by a more critical difference in the scene.

It was not exactly like a play, for there was no movement, no sound, and no speaking. The people were frozen in a tableau, arms raised, heads tipped back, as though they were all yelling though no words came out.

"What is this?" Elijah asked.

"Let us go in and see for ourselves," the Warrior of Old said quietly. He began to walk through the crowd, and Elijah followed him. It was like walking through a room of statues in a gallery, except that each person was undeniably real. No one moved as Elijah passed; all eyes were trained forward.

Elijah looked at the people he passed with increasing interest. Many seemed to be jeering and filled with interest, but others looked worried and serious. Not a hair moved in the room. He and the Warrior stepped out of the crowd at last, as one might step from a forest into a clearing. He looked up and saw that the portico was supported by two enormous pillars, as wide around as great oaks might be, and between those two enormous pillars was chained an enormous man. His head was down, shaved, and he seemed to be completely exhausted. There was a bandage tied about his eyes.

Elijah was about to ask his companion who the man was and how he came to be caught there, but as the words caught in his throat. For the man, unlike the rest of the motionless crowd, moved.

He lifted his head and took a great gasp of air, and cocked his head towards Elijah.

"You wish to know who I am?" he asked quietly.

Elijah looked around him in surprise. "I...I do," he said faltering. "And I wish to know where I am."

"You are in the Chamber of Strength," the chained man answered, straightening wearily. His arms could only fall part of the way to his sides, so strong were the chains. "And I am a man you have heard of all your life. I am Samson."

Elijah realized this was the Samson of the classic story of Samson and Delilah. He wasn't certain of the details; it was one of those Bible stories that popular culture had caught up and romanticized. He mostly knew that Samson had been a strong man with long hair, somehow blessed by God, but he had let himself be led astray by a woman who betrayed him and cut his hair, thereby stealing his strength.

He looked around. "Where is Delilah?" he asked.

"She is not here," Samson said. " I cannot see any longer, but I know that she is not here. In any case, she is not why you have come. You have come here to learn about the Spirit of Might. It fell upon me once, and you have come to see how it might fall upon you as well."

"I'm not sure that I want it," Elijah said frankly, looking around at the dismal scene. "I do not mean any disrespect, but it does not seem as though it might have served you well."

"It is no fault of the spirit," the man said with a wry laugh. "I know what it feels like to have the Strength of the Lord, and I gave it all up."

"What is it like?" Elijah asked.

"It is an overpowering force. It overcomes, it surpasses. It is extraordinary." A soft smile turned up his lips for only a moment. "I lost myself in Him. It wasn't my strength at all; it was the Lord's. I tore up a gate, bars and all, and carried it away on my shoulders. I defeated many enemies with no real weapon. I did things no other man had ever done because the Spirit of Might was upon me."

Elijah felt a sense of awe settle upon him at the words. He had seen power in his time, but never like what Samson was describing. He thought of the men he had considered strong before--men like Draxler, men who could knock a man out with a single punch, men who seemed in control of their life and their destiny. This was different. Samson wasn't talking about a power achieved by his own strength. He was talking about something that had been given to him, bestowed upon him. He talked of himself as if he was a vessel for something--Someone--greater.

"What happened?" Elijah looked around him. "What did they do to you? All this because of a woman?"

"My story is not about a woman," Samson said with that dry laugh again. It was a sad, sad sound. "My story is about what happens when the Spirit of Might leaves the one it had chosen."

"Tell him why the Spirit left you," the Warrior of Old said suddenly, his voice clear and loud.

Samson tilted his head to the side, unable to see where the voice was coming from but clearly interested. "Perhaps He grew displeased with me."

The Warrior walked forward and reached out, touching the bandage across Samson's eyes. The large man stood still beneath his hand. The Warrior of Old spoke quietly. "You were called for so much more than your strength alone," he said. "You were called to be the hand of justice and power, the vessel for miracles, signs, and wonders. You were called to fear the Lord and to stand in reverence of Him."

The large man began to weep, and Elijah realized that the attitude of exhaustion and weakness seemed to be leaving him even as the tears began running down his cheeks. He cried out in the voice of one who had lost everything, sobbing, but he seemed strangely stronger than he had moments before.

"The Spirit is returning," he said, leaning forward against the chains, leaning towards the Warrior of Old. He raised his head, his sightless eyes tilted towards Heaven, and cried out in a loud voice: "Lord, remember me. Strengthen me."

Elijah stepped back and saw that all around him, the people had moved from their frozen positions. He was in the middle of a throng of screaming, jeering people, listening to their calling for their false gods, and cry against the man bound between the pillars. He saw Samson reach out and put his hands on the marble on either side of himself and begin to push against it, straining.

He turned to the Warrior of Old, who had come to stand by his side. "What is he doing?" he asked.

The Warrior of Old didn't answer, but one of the strange men in the crowd yelled out, "Look at the Israelite. He thinks he can bring down an entire temple with only his hands."

Cruel laughter began to course through the crowd, but Elijah saw what the others had not yet realized. There were cracks in the marble pillars. Samson was straining, but at the last moment, he threw his head up towards Heaven and called out in an unintelligible voice before pushing one last time. The pillars cracked, and Elijah fell to the ground, covering his head in a hopeless attempt to save himself amid the sound of screams and disaster.

Suddenly, all was silent. He pulled his hands from his head and looked up. He was still standing in the enormous room, but only the Warrior of Old stood across from him. The portico, the pillars, the crowd, and the strong man were all gone. Only the lantern remained, and the dust particles dancing in it looked as beautiful as stars in a night sky.

Elijah stood on shaky legs.

"I don't understand," he said, trying to grasp the lesson. "You show me a man who had the Spirit of Might within him, but his ending was so gruesome, his time on Earth tainted by his own mistakes."

"Samson had only part of the vision," the Warrior of Old said, leaning on his staff. "He understood and enjoyed the power, but he grew distracted and distant from the source of that power. He began to rely on himself, and his heart was not in a posture that knelt to the One who had given him the might in the first place. You have the chance to do better, Elijah."

"I?" Elijah asked, laughing despite himself. "You cannot be serious. That man was filled with the supernatural power of God. Of course, he could do all those things. He had something special. I am not like that. I am not like him."

"Haven't you heard anything I have taught you?" the Warrior of Old said in mild exasperation. "It does not matter if you are anything like *him*. The Might does not come from *him*, it comes from the Spirit, and that same Spirit can live and dwell within all those who know Christ. Think of His servant, Paul, who said that he bows his knees to the King, from whom the whole family in Heaven and Earth is named. He says that from that King, you may be strengthened with His Might by His Spirit in the inner places of your heart."

"Samson had the Spirit of Might for a time," Elijah said quietly, his heart sober. "I want to live a life filled with the Strength and Might of the Lord so that I can serve Christ. I know that I need it to live fully, but I don't want to make the same mistakes Samson did. I don't want to wake up and find myself one day chained by my own pride."

The Warrior of Old nodded. "It is wise of you to recognize this. Before we walk on to the next chamber, you must allow me to give you something that I gave to Samson in the end--something that will aid in your stewardship of the Spirit of Might."

Elijah nodded, waiting. The Warrior of Old walked forward, his hand reaching to lay on Elijah's shoulder.

"I give to you, as an aid in your newfound might, the Spirit of Reverence and fear of the Lord," he said. He spoke in a voice as low and soft as a mother might speak when talking to her child, and yet the words rumbled in Elijah's heart like a thunderstorm on the horizon. He expected to feel a kind of power in his veins, a strength in his joints and tendons, but instead, he felt his knees drawn to the ground as though by an invisible force, and all he could think about was the man who had saved him from the well, the Son of Father God, the King of Kings, Christ Jesus.

The Spirit of Might and the Spirit of the Fear of the Lord were less like a call to battle and more like a call back to First Love. He felt the tears in his own eyes that he had seen in Samson's, and he knew in part what real might felt like. The fear of the Lord had left room for no other fear in his life.

Elijah thought of the things he had been most terrified of on Earth, and he felt like laughing. Fear had controlled more than he ever knew. It had kept him from loving his wife the way he ought to have. It had kept him from honesty and truth and the community of believers. It had kept him from looking for an adventure in the Kingdom because he had been afraid of disappointment. It had even kept him from facing his own darkness because he had been afraid of ending up so deep, like Charlie, that he could not escape.

Now he saw that the fear of the Lord and a reverence for the King drove out all other fears, and he felt all at once humbled and invincible.

He stood and faced the Warrior of Old. "Thank you," he said quietly, bowing his head.

"Now you are ready for the second chamber," the Warrior of Old smiled. "Walk with me into the Chamber of Wisdom, and we shall see what the King is preparing for you there."

Chapter Ten

The Chamber of Wisdom

Elijah halted in the doorway, startled at the scene inside. It was another hall of sorts, but entirely different from the one they had just left. The ceilings were low and irregular, with various intricate angles to accommodate what appeared to be multiple hearths and furnaces about the room. It was warm and loud, the crashing of metal against metal met his ears, and the sound of water hissing near at hand.

It took Elijah a moment to realize that he was standing in a blacksmithery, but this was nothing like the rudimentary shops and shacks he had seen in historical movies. This was a grand room--a place where things of worth and power were created. He could feel the majesty of it all.

"Now here's a lad I didn't expect to see today," came a booming voice from one side of the room.

Elijah gave a start and turned to see that he and the Warrior of Old were not alone in the chamber. Four men stood together around a drawing of sorts spread on a small wooden table in the corner, each strong and rough and wizened. The more outspoken of the four, a red-headed chap with muscles like cords and a twinkle in his eye, was the one who had called out to Elijah. The other three left the table and set about different tasks around the room as their friend spoke, but Elijah could see that they were closely watching the conversation.

"Do I know you?" Elijah asked slowly. He wondered if they were also characters from the Bible, as the paintings and Samson had been.

"Just the right question, if I do say so myself," the red-headed man tipped his head back and laughed deeply. He strode forward, crossing what seemed like a large expanse with only a few strides, and extended a hand to Elijah in the greeting of a brother and a friend. "I am the Spirit of Knowledge," he said.

Elijah was taken aback. The Spirit of Might and the Spirit of the Fear of the Lord had been bestowed upon him from the Warrior of Old. They had been powerful but invisible blessings. Here was a Spirit personified in the flesh before him. He turned and looked at the Warrior of Old and saw a new affection in his eyes. He shrugged when he caught Elijah looking at him.

"They are family," he said simply. Then he stepped forward and embraced the red-haired man. "Show my friend what it is you are working on today."

The Spirit of Knowledge nodded curtly and strode over to the forge at one end of the room. He positioned himself across from the bellows and fanned the flames before taking a rod of shimmering metal out of a case and thrusting it deep into the coals.

The Warrior of Old followed, explaining to Elijah as he went. "The Spirit of Knowledge is practiced at gathering facts and information from around the world. He is always in a state of preparation. He takes his time, never overlooking anything-- setting aside the concerns of frail earthly things and filling his mind with information."

"I cannot tell what he is making," Elijah said, watching the metal begin to glow before his eyes.

"You wouldn't, not yet anyway," the Warrior of Old said with a gentle laugh. "The Spirit of Knowledge is not so focused on the finished product. He is a gatherer, a bringer-in of information. He needs his brothers to make all that knowledge useful.

"He needs me, is what you mean." Another deep voice spoke at Elijah's elbow, and he turned to see that another of the four had come to stand near at hand. This man's skin was dark as ebony, and his eyes were laughing and bright. He seemed young and full of life, but when Elijah looked at him, he saw the elegance and wisdom of old age. He wore a thick leather apron over his garments and had wide forearm guards attached to his gloves.

He reached into the flames, smiling at the Spirit of Knowledge with brotherly affection, and retrieved the metal rod with a pair of iron clamps.

"Come with me," he said, turning with the quiet confidence of someone who knew he would be followed.

They left the forge and walked to an anvil. Elijah watched as the giant of a man began to hammer away at the rod with great, violent strokes. At first, it seemed like brutish work, but as the process progressed, Elijah saw the man return again and again to the red-haired man and the forge, putting the bar into the flames and then pulling it out and working more and more delicately on the shape of the thing. It grew flat and long.

As he worked, he kept looking up at the Warrior of Old and

[107]

asking for advice. Elijah watched this with interest. He could see an apparent affection between the blacksmith and his companion, but he could also see that they were taking their orders from the Warrior, that he had some responsibility in this great forge as well.

"This is the Spirit of Wisdom," the Warrior of Old explained to Elijah at intervals in the process. "He has the most natural talent of anyone here, as you can see. He has the gift of sight to see the finished product even before it is complete and takes care of the work before him. He takes the raw materials of what the Spirit of Knowledge brings him and fashions something powerful."

Elijah noticed the third man, wiry and slight, had come to stand beside the Spirit of Wisdom and watched with interest with bright eyes.

"And him?" he asked. "I would have guessed him to be the one with the gift of sight."

"That is the Spirit of Understanding," the Warrior of Old answered. "He has his own work to do, but he is always watching the work of Knowledge and Wisdom to find ways to put it into his own actions and everyday life. He is the most practical of them all."

At that moment, the Spirit of Wisdom transferred the weapon he was working on, now obviously a sword, into the possession of the Spirit of Understanding, who took it back to be heated again and then began to bury the sword in what looked to be a barrel of sand.

"What is he doing?" Elijah asked.

"He is cooling it slowly, so it will be ready for the Spirit of Counsel."

Elijah turned and saw that the oldest of the four men, a tall man with a white beard and bright blue eyes, had approached the barrel and was waiting to retrieve the sword. When the time had come, at last, he pulled it out and took it over to a grinder at the far end of the room. The sound was deafening--sparks flew as he went to work, and the sword flashed sharper and brighter than before.

When the noise had died down, at last, the Spirit of Counsel took the object in his hands to a long table in the center of the room. The other three spirits gathered around him, making changes, comparing to the original design papers, and arguing good-naturedly with one another.

"The Spirit of Counsel aids the other three in every way he can," the Warrior of Old said quietly. "He informs the decisions of Wisdom, Knowledge, and Understanding with the steadiness of Wise Counsel. He is the final polishing and sharping of the work of the other three. This is the partnership of the four."

They drew near the group crowded around the table. Elijah listened to their conversation with amusement. They reminded him of the other meaningful brotherhoods in his life--the men he had fought with, the others at the gym, even his own friendship with Daniel.

"It's not bad," Wisdom was saying, "but perhaps we should have cooled it slower."

"You're only saying that because you don't like us to rush into action before you've determined the absolute result," Understanding said with a guffaw. "If it were up to you, we would be pounding iron for an eternity, and we would never be able to use our tools in the real world."

"You're just showing off for the new guy," Knowledge said, nodding at Elijah.

"Says the man who felt the need to use the bellows even though he'd already heated his coals earlier," Wisdom retorted with a good-natured laugh.

The teasing diminished somewhat, and they talked earnestly of the changes they wanted to make and how the weapon's balance was set. Elijah could see that there was great respect between the four of them. It made him long for that sort of community in his own life.

"They need each other," the Warrior of Old said as if reading his thoughts. "Knowledge is a good thing to have, but he must have Wisdom from above to direct his purpose, and Wisdom must have Understanding to put all this into action. Understanding, in turn, must be open to Counsel and direction along the way."

He stepped forward, and the four men respectfully parting, letting the oldest examine the sword. Elijah wanted to look at it himself, but they hid his view of it.

"It will need a bit more polishing," the Spirit of Counsel said quietly. "But it will be ready in time."

The Warrior of Old nodded and drew back. "We will be waiting," he said.

Then he turned back to Elijah, who asked, "May I see it?"

"No," he said, "not yet. But the time will come, I assure you. There is an element of the Chamber of Wisdom that is only given and not achieved. You must try to put into practice the skills you have seen here today, but the Spirit of Wisdom, Understanding, Counsel, and Knowledge will travel with you and advise you along the remainder of this journey to give aid where needed."

Hearing that, Elijah half expected the four men to follow them on their journey, but the Warrior of Old was the only one that walked with him to the door. They opened the door and stepped out, closing the great oaken doors behind them.

They stepped into a small hall of sorts, clearing a holding room for the more splendid destination beyond. Elijah saw, a few paces away, the entrance to a Third Chamber. This was a great door, almost two stories tall, made of gilded metals, and embedded with a few bright jewels along with the handle. Elijah drew a deep breath at the sight of it.

"It's beautiful," he said. "What is the Third Chamber?"

"All will be revealed in due time," the Warrior of Old answered, "but first, I want to speak about all you have seen. Thus far, you have met with six of the seven spirits of God: The Spirit of Might, fear of the Lord, Wisdom, Knowledge, Understanding, and Counsel."

"What is the seventh Spirit?" Elijah asked.

"It awaits you in the final chamber: The Throne Room." The Warrior of Old's eyes were enlightened with joy and reverence. "The seven spirits are all of the Holy Spirit, every child of the King--including yourself, ought to walk in the fullness of the Spirit."

"I have never heard of seven spirits," Elijah said quietly. "Daniel spoke of the Holy Spirit many times in church, but these seven sounds strange and foreign."

The Warrior of Old laughed. "I assure you, I have no desire to draw you away from true theology. The seven spirits are manifestations of the Holy Spirit, the One who should be leading and guiding you through your daily walk. It bears distinguishing because some believers walk tentatively, only embracing Wisdom on occasion, or perhaps Understanding, but not understanding the fullness available to them. When the seven attributes are functioning in your life, you will be balanced with the Spirit of the Lord and the Spirit of Might. You'll be full of the Word because of the Spirit of Wisdom, Knowledge, Understanding, and Counsel. Finally, the Spirit of the Fear of the Lord will balance all these with humility, and you will avoid the pitfall of becoming puffed up before God."

Elijah felt an eagerness rising within him. "The seventh Spirit, then, is this Spirit of the Lord?"

The Warrior of Old nodded his head. "Now, it is time for you to walk with me into the third and final chamber--the last stop before you must face the Dark One."

Elijah felt the old stab of fear at the words, but something about the expression in the Warrior of Old's face kept his panic at bay.

It was challenging to be truly frightened of anything in the presence of such a companion, with all he had already learned.

"What is the final chamber?" he asked.

"The most amazing one of all," the Warrior of Old said, pushing at the great door in front of them and stepping back as it swung open. "It is the Throne Room."

Chapter Eleven

The Throne Room

Whatever shred of fear or confusion, Elijah had felt at the mention of the Dark One disappeared entirely when he stepped into that room. He wondered as he looked around if he could even call it a room. There were walls, a ceiling and a floor and windows, and a dais, yet it seemed vast as an outdoor arena or an open field on a summer day.

He caught his breath and froze in the doorway, unsure if he even deserved to walk on that grand, golden, translucent floor. It stretched out before him like glass, shimmering and smooth and unmarred, pouring forward to the raised station at the far end of the room where a great Throne was erected.

It was a place of activity, life, and light. There were dimensions to the room that Elijah had not seen anywhere else in the castle--levels, balconies, ladders going up and down and out of the great chamber, and upon all these levels brilliant robed beings were hurrying along, talking together, and turning always and again towards the Throne. There was laughter in the room: great, stately laughter like that of nobles before their King, soft, delighted laughter like that of a child at the feet of the father.

There was activity in the room, but there was also rest. Large groups of the beautiful robed beings that Elijah had guessed were angels gathered around the Throne in an attitude of attentiveness, and even those who hurried in and out with messages seemed to do so in a way that centered around the dais, as though even their service was an act of worship.

The robed beings were so beautiful Elijah could hardly look at them. They had forms like humans but seemed different somehow. Light came steadily from them, and yet Elijah knew it was not their own light. They were small, twinkling stars compared to the great sun of the Throne, and once Elijah's eyes centered on that dais, he found it impossible to look away.

Out from the base of the platform, and winding around it, he saw that the ground was moving, the glass twinkling at the feet of the Throne. It took Elijah a moment to understand that the space between the floor and the Throne were divided by a flowing river. It was unlike any Elijah has ever seen before. This river seemed to be living, filled with the shimmer of refracting light as if he was looking at clear, flowing crystals.

A distinct sound came out of the waters--the healing sound that reflected the joy of Heaven and the frequency of life. On closer examination, Elijah realized that there were streams within streams, a river within a river within a river. He couldn't tell where one began, and the other ended, but he felt that the longer he looked at the streams, the more the distinction didn't matter. The strength of the river was tied to the source, and Elijah knew without asking the Warrior of Old that the river's source was the heart of the King Himself.

The beauty of the Throne Room seemed to captivate time: a moment expanded into eternity. The only focal point that could even stand to overcome this moment was the glory of the Throne. It was great and noble and beautiful, and it too moved like it was alive. Elijah had the distinct feeling that it was like peering into the sun when he looked at the Throne, the light blazing and white and pure. It was so bright he couldn't see if there was even a figure upon it--when he looked directly at it, there seemed to be one Throne, but when he looked away, for the briefest of moments, he thought there were three thrones one beside the other. And by the Throne and the river was an altar burning incense.

"It smells wonderful," Elijah said.

"The incense is the prayers of the saints and intercession of the King, which is a sweet-smelling savor to Father God," explained the Warrior of Old.

He turned to the Warrior of Old at his side. "It is beautiful," he said. "Is that the Throne of the King?"

"It is," the Warrior of Old answered him.

"Will we meet the King?" Elijah asked, his knees feeling suddenly weak.

"You have already met Him," the Warrior of Old answered. Then, with a smile, "and you have yet to meet Him."

Elijah thought back to the figure that loomed largest in his adventures thus far. "The Son?" he asked. "Jesus is the King?"

"He is, and more holy and wonderful than you can yet imagine. Still, if you look around this room, you may well feel another presence here, weighty and glorious." The Warrior of Old looked at him with a twinkle in his eye. "The Father God is very present, very real, and very strong. He transcends the universe. He is everywhere."

Elijah frowned. "If He is everywhere, is He really a person like Daniel used to say? If He transcends the universe, how can He be at all someone to love or who could love in return?"

"There is a mystery here that is too deep for words," the Warrior of Old answered. "But it is a mystery worth learning for the rest of time. I will say that Father God looks down on His Creation and His Son with love, and His thoughts for you outnumber the sea. He is holy beyond measure, and yet personally invested in your individual story."

"And the Throne? Whose is it?" Elijah asked, catching the trick of the light again, uncertain if it was three thrones or one.

"It is His, and it is Theirs," the Warrior of Old answered cryptically. "Think of understanding in this matter as if you were shown color in the grand universe. Imagine that someone showed you a sliver of scarlet, and you stared at it until you fully understood it. You would be entranced, certainly, but you would not know until you had been shown the fullness of a prism exposed to infinite light and, therefore, infinite color. The full revelation of the mystery of the Godhead will be learning that encompasses eternity. For now, take in what you can and let the overflow pour into you like water."

The Warrior of Old did not let him linger long in this reverie but instead, put a hand on his elbow and urged him forward.

"Come into the light," he said.

Elijah could not. That ground seemed too holy, and a thick emotion clouded his thoughts. He had never been in a place like this before. He had never even had the context to imagine such beauty. Only one thing did he know with any certainty: "I do not belong here," he said in broken tones, pulling back from the Warrior of Old and edging away from the door.

Before the Warrior of Old could respond, there was a

movement at the other end of the room that caught Elijah's attention and held him transfixed.

Elijah felt his breath catch in his throat as a man stood and moved away from the light of the Throne, coming out in blazing glory to stand upon the dais. There was a shimmering light around Him that cast prisms of color across the room, and all the figures--both angels and people--waved like wheat in the wind at the movement of His presence. He had captured everyone the way he'd captured Elijah. Every eye was on him, every knee shivered down into a prostrate bow at the sight of him. Elijah's own heart thudded heavily in his chest as he knelt to the ground.

He wanted to bow his head, but he couldn't remove his eyes from the glory of the figure. The man was tall, with long white robes that fell from his shoulders to the ground, gilded with gold. Elijah remembered seeing an opal once on Earth, what seemed like years ago, and he remembered the way the gem had seemed both purely white and shimmering with color at the same time. It was a paltry comparison in the light of this glory, but it helped him understand what he saw. He was filled with fear and trembled, and yet he wanted more than anything to be near that man even though he could not find the courage within himself to make the journey across the Throne Room.

The man walked down the dais, moved across the river as though it were land, and then began to make his way towards Elijah.

It was then that the rhythm of Elijah's heart changed with a shock of recognition. The man before him--the King who had left His Throne and come down to meet with Elijah--was none other than the Son who had saved him from the well. The glory was still there in its entirety, but somehow, inexplicably, Elijah felt the personal love of the man as he came closer. He felt like a son that had been gone from home for many years, returning to the faithful love of a father. It was a strange feeling, for Elijah had no reference point from which to understand a father's, pure love. Yet there it was, nonetheless.

The eyes of the Son were fixed on him, and he kept coming across the vast expanse, a relentless, all-seeing force that made Elijah both desperate to go to him and desperate to flee. Every time he thought of running away, those eyes of love held him. Every time he thought of moving forward, he was overcome by the understanding that the Son, the King, was wholly pure and that Elijah's unworthiness stood out in stark contrast to that purity.

The King was almost to him. Elijah saw something flash amid the white robes and realized what he saw: dark wounds in the perfect man's hands and feet. He dropped his eyes, overcome with the love of Christ in the face of his own self-condemnation.

The King stopped in front of Elijah.

"My Elijah, welcome," he said, with a voice as strong as thunder and as light as laughter.

"I cannot," Elijah said. His knees felt weak, and he realized that even if he had felt worthy, he would not have had the strength to approach that flaming Throne. "I do not belong to this place."

"You belong because I have deemed you worthy," the king-man said. Elijah raised his gaze at last. Jesus' eyes were like fire. "You may approach the Throne because I am walking beside you. All of my children can freely come to the Throne. It is not just about you but all that is divinely appointed to be in your path Elijah, and yet because I have chosen *you*, it is all about you."

"I don't understand," Elijah said, sucking in his breath. "You came down into the well to rescue me--you saw everything that is in my past and perhaps even what is in my future, and you still think that someone as filthy as I deserve to cross that pristine floor and approach the Throne? I know that you are Jesus, I have heard of grace, but I do not understand it. All I know is that if I walk before the Throne in this condition, I will be burned alive."

The face of Jesus was full of tenderness. "When I died for you on the cross," he said, "your sins were nailed with me, and my blood set you free. You can walk forward to the Throne in confidence under that covering."

"My sins?" Elijah asked, confused. "You mean the sins of all humanity. I know you died on the cross for everyone. You gave your life to save everyone."

Jesus smiled, his eyes full of joy. "If it had been only you, Elijah, I would have done the same thing." He took a step forward, his gaze holding Elijah captive. "I know everything there is to know about you. I perceive every movement of your heart and soul, and I know every thought before it even enters your mind. I have gone into your future to prepare the way, and in kindness, I follow behind you to spare you the harm of your past. I died not for men, but for each man."

"But not for me alone..." Elijah began in amazement.

"For the joy set before me, I endured the cross, and if had been only your heart set before me, you would have been joy enough." He looked at the Warrior of Old as though they shared some secret knowledge. "Think of the stories I told--the lost sheep, the lost coin, the prodigal son--they are all about how one is willing to leave everything to search for one lost soul. I died for the world, but I also died for you personally."

"Elijah," Jesus continued, "before my Father laid down Earth's foundations, He had you in mind. You were the focus of Our love, to make you whole and holy by Our love."

"How do you know I was worth it?" Elijah asked, his heart full. "What if you paid a high price for the wrong soul?"

"I do not make mistakes," Jesus went on. "I know you were worth it because I paid a high price for you. I told you what your value was when I died on the cross for you." He waved across the room at someone Elijah could not see. "My servant and friend, Paul, grasped this concept perfectly when he recognized he was the least in the Kingdom, while also acknowledging that my sacrifice gave him boldness to walk before the Throne, and free access as kings before the Father because of his confidence in My faithfulness."

Elijah's mind began to understand, but his heart could not. He could see that this boldness was not in contrast to humility, but he was still afraid to step before the Throne. He turned to Jesus. "I want to," he said. "I want to repent of everything I have done and stand before you with confidence, but I don't know how."

"It is a mysterious and wonderful thing that your confidence and boldness relies on me," Jesus said. "You cannot even understand the grace and love you have been given until I provide you a heart that can receive it, but that is no obstacle for me. I am here to give you love and joy that overflows as the living water which overflowed from the well of your heart. Let my love be a resting place for you, the source and root of your life from here on forward. Don't fight anymore against it and hold up your own worthiness or unworthiness--those things don't matter anymore. You are worthy because I have declared you worthy. You are loved because I have declared you loved. You are empowered because I have declared you empowered."

At that moment, the words of King Jesus took a life of their own. They flowed out of His mouth and became flesh within Elijah. One spoken Word from Jesus healed a lifetime of scaring from the access points of the Dark One.

He brought forth another garment and presented it to Elijah. It was glorious, full of colors Elijah had never seen before, and radiated power and love.

"Son," Jesus said, "You wear the garment of my identity. It looks so good on you, Elijah. Let us activate the threads of praise, for this is a weapon against the feeling of unworthiness."

The Garment of Christ began to shine like sunlight at dawn. It emanated from him because it is becoming a part of him. Elijah wept, and every tear that fell washed him with the truth, and the Word of Life penetrated his innermost being. From the most profound parts of Elijah's soul came a noise so pure, so powerful, so glorious it surprised even him. Praise poured out of Elijah.

Jesus reached out, put His hand on Elijah's shoulder, and said, "Never doubt again who you are. Rest in me and now receive the beauty of the deeper levels of praise within you, be filled with my joy, and my garment will always protect you from the Dark One ever sending his spirit of despair to harm you again."

And at that moment, Elijah regained his strength to stand. And with this, Jesus said, "The threads of praise are the source of your Joy and my Strength, I also call forth the threads of humility to increase."

Elijah was in awe, marveling that he should be called to walk by the side of such a One. He had never known a man who could embrace both meekness and courage, yet here the One he respected above all others was inviting him to experience full humility along with full boldness before the Throne. He stepped forward, engulfed in the deeper activations of the Garment of Christ in him and with the revelation that this garment will be the source of continued instruction as one walks as an overcomer.

The floor felt light and smooth under Elijah's feet. He began to look around and saw that the Throne Room witnesses were also filled with light, but unlike the angels, they changed as he and the Son and the Warrior of Old passed by. They were like living paintings. As he looked at them, he saw glimpses of their lives on Earth, though their faces were continually pointed towards the King and then towards the Throne.

"They are the saints," Jesus said as they walked, noting Elijah's attention. "They can stand before the Throne as you do now. They are the champions that came before you who experienced great victory for me, sometimes in the most difficult of situations."

Elijah watched, and before his eyes saw as if in a vision, some of what these people had endured. Old patriarchal characters were battling the wilderness, some being mocked and beaten, others who were going through atrocities that he had only heard of, for the sake of their faith. He noticed these things as one might see a shadow--it was hard to focus too much on what had been endured in the light of what had been gained. The cloud of witnesses around the Throne seemed wholly engaged in the beauty before them, not in the shadows of their past sufferings, and yet Elijah knew those sufferings mattered when he turned and saw the face of the Son beside him. Jesus' eyes were full of tears.

"Some of my children walked through great pain and loss," he said in broken tones. "Following me is not easy. Even for you, Elijah, there will be many trials ahead, some brought upon by the Enemy himself. But hear me," he paused, his feet stopping for a moment in his forward motion so that he could reach out and put his hands on Elijah's arms and compel his full attention. "This is the path to hope when it appears that all hope is lost. No person can hurt you, for even in death, you will enter eternity with me. Remember all that you have learned on this journey and walk with the Spirit of the Lord. This will unlock everything to you--all strength and wisdom needed to do my will. Rejoice in your sufferings, Elijah, for with a surrendered heart, you can be trusted with the world. Seek first my Kingdom and my Righteousness, and I will not only take care of all your needs, but I will always provide for my Kingdom advancements through your calling."

"What do I need to do to serve you?" Elijah asked. He had served many masters before meeting this man, but now he knew in his heart that the reason he couldn't find fulfillment on Earth was that he was pouring all his energies into serving things that had no eternal value. This was a man he could follow. This was a man he could love.

Jesus smiled. "That's the beauty of it. Continue to be a vessel into which I can pour my love, strategies, and plans. I have called you a Mighty Warrior, and now it is for you to walk in the confidence of new life in me. It is as I spoke to my servant Matthew: all power is given unto me in Heaven and on Earth, so you are to go and teach to all nations and baptize in the name of the Father and the Son and the Holy Ghost." He released Elijah, but his eyes still held him fast. "So often people hear that commission and begin to go and do immediately--trying to spread my Name and the Name of my Father throughout the Earth and earn a place in my Kingdom, but they forget that they need only allow themselves to be loved by me, and to love me in return. This is the starting place. Find me in the secret place. I will provide the Wisdom and Strength for the plan I will set before you. All will always be provided for the advancement of my Kingdom."

Jesus turned and began walking as He spoke to Elijah, "Come and let the virtue of joy fill you, the spirit of despair can no longer have victory over you when My garment is on." Elijah noticed as Jesus spoke, the threads of the garment radiated the truth of comfort and joy throughout his being. It was like oil penetrating his skin and warmed his heart. A wave of gratefulness washed over Elijah. This very moment was set before he was ever born, in the place of eternity. For this moment, the Creator of the Universe, the vastness of space, had made way for Elijah and a path to full adoption into this heavenly family provided by the King of Kings. If nothing else was done for Elijah, he would give praise from a place of eternal gratitude.

The three--the Warrior of Old, Elijah, and Jesus--stopped a few feet away from the dais and the Throne. Elijah was ready now-- walking in his new understanding of identity and eager to meet the Father at last, but as he moved to put his foot on the lower step, he heard a voice from above him, soft and rumbling like thunder, interrupting him.

"My son," the voice said, gentle and firm. "There is yet something you must face before your knighting ceremony and before you approach the Throne."

It was the voice of Father God. Elijah knew it without explanation by the way his heart quaked within him. "Your Son said that I am forgiven, that I am clean," he said. "What more is there for me to repent?"

"My son, man's nature continues to carry the sins of generations long before him, which include sins man were so willing to take upon themselves. You carry both. What you are being shown is a path to freedom from sin and death. The path is made straight through continually surrendering to my Son, who defeated sin and death. Once internal darkness is revealed to you, this is your right provided by my Son to renounce and turn away from the agreements you have made with the Enemy. Repentance is the way to continued righteousness. Love is the result. Therefore, a lack of love for your earthly father is evidence of the Enemy's work in you. This is what troubles your soul." Father God said.

Elijah turned in confusion to Jesus, and in response, the beautiful man nodded ever so slightly and held out a hand to invite him to walk over to a nearby door of sorts set up to the side of the dais. Elijah felt a moment of resistance. He had come this far, was so near the Throne, and was ready to stand upon the dais and walk in his calling at last. Why should he be derailed from that mission? Still, the eyes of the Son called to him, and he could not but answer.

"What does He mean?" Elijah asked Jesus. "What must I repent for?"

"There is a matter of unforgiveness still to be settled in your heart," Jesus said.

"Still?" Elijah thought of the spiders and the access points. In many ways, they seemed to be an ago long memory compared to the glory all around him, but still, he could recall the fear of that battle. "I thought I had already moved past that unforgiveness. Some people injured me in the past, but I let that bitterness go."

Jesus' eyes were kind. Elijah thought, as he looked into them, that he had never known eyes like that on Earth--kindness strong as a weapon that sliced through to the core of his being. "Your unforgiveness towards your father shackles you still, and it makes it difficult for you to connect with your Heavenly Father."

Elijah shook his head. "I let all of that go," he said. "I don't need to forgive him because I have removed him from memory. Besides, he left me as a child, he hurt my mother, my family, my brother, but he can't hurt me anymore." He shrugged. "I'm not even mad at him. He has no effect on me." He thought of all the times when he had answered Daniel's gentle questions by assuring him that if their father had walked into the room at that moment, he could have easily ignored the man. "I don't consider him my father. I haven't for the longest time. He means nothing to me."

"My son, it is time to release this way of thinking. You are protecting yourself, but it will only cause a root of bitterness to grow in you," King Jesus said quietly. "Also, Elijah, he may be nothing to you, but he is something to me."

Elijah looked at him in disbelief. The bitter taste of rejection echoed in his heart.

"I said once that you should pray for your enemies," the Son said, his eyes shining tenderly. "Do you know why I said that?"

Elijah shook his head, his mind spinning.

"When you pray for your enemies, there is a forgiveness process that occurs," Jesus explained. "Even indifference turns to affection over time. Indifference is as strong as hatred, my son."

Elijah felt Jesus' hand on his shoulder and turned to see that what he had thought was a door was, in fact, a canvas draped between two poles. There was a painting on the canvas, just as there had been in the Corridor of Champions and in the center of the fighting ring where Elijah had faced the access points. The painting on this larger canvas was frozen at first but came to life when the Son reached out and touched it with his fingers.

In the painting, a little boy--perhaps three or four years of age--was cowering in a closet. His clothes were worn, his haircut slicked back and old-fashioned. He was shaking. Elijah could hear, though he couldn't see, the sounds of an argument outside the door of the closet. He could see tears on the little boy's face.

"What is this?" he asked, his heart going out to the child.

There was no answer at first, but as he watched, the closet door flung open, and a hand dragged the boy out of the frame of the painting. The boy cried out, and Elijah felt the sudden urge to leap through the painting and rescue him. He could do nothing. He turned, upset, and looked into the compassionate face of the King at his side.

"Your father," Jesus explained.

Elijah started, then looked again, more closely. He had never seen pictures of his father as a child, but he trusted his companion. It was strange to see someone he had considered to be a perpetrator all his life now cowering before him as the victim. There was no victory in it. Elijah felt sick for the little boy in the painting.

"He never talked about his past," he said quietly.

"Many people don't," the Warrior of Old interjected. "Especially when the past looks like this."

The Son nodded in acknowledgment. "I want you to see your father the way I see him. I love the little boy, and I love the grown man. I hate what he did to you and your brother, but I see the end from the beginning and the beginning from the end. I see what trauma is hidden in the corners of his heart."

Elijah felt that cold in different parts of his heart, beginning to shake within him, and he crossed his arms across his chest.

"No," he said, pushing back against this revelation. "I can't do it. I can't just turn away from all the pain that my father caused and pretend it's gone. I can't forget what he did to me and what he did to the ones I love. He was a coward." He began to shake at the memories. "I don't want to do this," he said. "I don't want to feel this pain." It had been so much easier when it was just him and his indifference, but it seemed that forgiveness could only happen with feeling. Jesus reached out then and put his hand squarely on Elijah's chest, directly over his heart. The touch felt like searing fire, and at first, Elijah cried out in surprise, but in the next instant, he realized it wasn't precisely pain he was experiencing--it was feeling. A part of him, long frozen, thawed in the light of the man before him, and tears sprang unbidden into his eyes.

"The root of bitterness gave you a heart of stone," Jesus said with quiet joy, "and I give you a heart of flesh. Don't be afraid of the pain associated with this forgiveness because I give you a living heart, full of the Spirit that is strong enough to face the past without getting drawn back into old fears and mistakes. I give you a soft heart that can look on your father with the compassion needed to understand My love for him."

Elijah gasped, stepping backward as tears began to run down his face. He wanted to process all of this, to understand the changes that were overrunning him. But before he did, the Son reached out again and touched the painting, changing the scene once more.

The scene before Elijah was now that of an old man in a dark, unadorned room. It looked generic, like the sort of place someone might board in at a halfway house, or perhaps even the corner of a homeless shelter. The walls were beige, there was a bunk bed, and the man sat upon it with his head down. Elijah looked at him and knew at once it was his father.

"Why are you showing me this?" he asked tears in his eyes. "Is he alive?"

"He is on Earth with you now," the Son said, his own eyes filled with compassion. "But he is not yet alive in Me. I'm showing you this for the sake of your own freedom, that you can see your father the way I see him. He is a child, a son, a broken man that I love as much as the purest of saints." He looked soberly at Elijah. "I also wish you to look on him as a father deserves to be seen, with love and respect."

Respect. It was a word Elijah knew well from his time in the gym and in the military. It was something he had fought for and something he only gave grudgingly to others. He had undoubtedly never viewed his father with anything close to respect, and perhaps without the One standing beside him, he would never be able to. Still, as he looked at the Warrior of Old in the painting, his heart broke within him. He wanted desperately to love that man in the way a son ought to love his father, with tenderness and honor.

"There is one last person you must forgive, even as you forgive your father," Jesus said, his hand moving back to Elijah's chest. "You have reached a place where you can have compassion for your father, and lastly, you must reach a place where you can have the same compassion for yourself. You know your every thought and weakness, and so you continue to hold onto judgment against yourself even when those you trust most accept you." He smiled with perfect understanding. "I know what you have said to yourself when you sit in my house and listen to your brother teach or when you are around those who profess my name. You believe that if they really knew the deepest parts of your heart, they would be disgusted by you-- you have not forgiven yourself."

He pulled back his hand, but the heat remained. "You must remember the lesson taught earlier, my friend. I have forgiven you, so you have no reason to withhold that forgiveness from yourself or others. I have seen the deepest and darkest parts of you, and I have washed you clean."

Elijah broke, then. He had been fracturing in a thousand beautiful lines ever since he'd stepped into the Throne Room, but this last movement of love, and the invitation to join forever in that love towards himself and others, destroyed him. He found himself swept up in the love as though it was a tangible thing, like rushing wind or a wave of inescapable water. He knelt and lowered his head into the strength of it, and when the initial power of the love abated enough for him to raise his head again, he could think of only one thing. He wanted to pour out all that had been poured into him: to the Warrior of Old, the Father, the Son, his family, and even onto his father.

"I forgive him," he said aloud, though it seemed redundant. He knew that Jesus already understood his forgiveness even before he spoke it. "I want to find him when this is all over. I want him to know that I see him the way You see him."

"My son," came the voice of Father God, full of joy. "Come and approach the Throne at last."

Chapter Twelve

The Knighting Ceremony

As Elijah walked forward, he noticed the shining river around the base of the Throne again. Up close, it was even more beautiful, skipping deep and clear across silver stones. It rushed eagerly along, like everything in the Throne Room. Elijah came to a stop at the edge of the river, raising his eyes to the Father. Jesus paused a moment beside him.

"I have more to say to you," he said, "but it is more than you can bear at this time. I will give you over to the Spirit of Truth, and he will guide you as you move forward. He will speak what he hears from the Father, and he will make known to you the mysteries that are before us. There will be times of grief ahead of you, dear one," he said with real tenderness in his voice, "but there will be the glory as well. Go forth and show the love that you have been given."

He turned, then, and waded quickly across the river, his robes caught up in the swirling current for a moment before he climbed out on the other side and stood beside the Father, glowing in the brilliant light of the Throne.

The Warrior of Old came and stood quietly beside Elijah in the place the Son had left. "Before you approach the Throne," he said gently, "you must be baptized in the river of life."

Elijah followed in awe into the water. His heart was still overcome with the love that had been shown to him. It rushed around his waist, and he felt as though he might be swept away in it. Before he was, the Warrior of Old came beside him and helped to hold him steady in the current.

The Warrior of Old placed his hands upon Elijah's head and chest and, speaking in a language Elijah did not know or understand, submerged him in the river. The water was clear, refreshing, and cleansing. Elijah felt he could have stayed beneath it for all eternity, and when he was pulled back up out of it, he could feel the power of the waters of life still clinging to him like a shimmering garment.

He opened his mouth to speak and from his tongue spilled a language that was not his own and that he did not understand. He was speaking to the Warrior of Old--or more accurately, **with** the Warrior of Old. They spoke together as they climbed out of the water, and Elijah knew they were speaking a prayer to the Father and his Son.

He stepped out on the dais and stood before King Jesus. He understood all in a moment why it was necessary to forgive his father and himself first, for Elijah knew as he looked into those eyes of fire--those eyes filled with the love of a Father--that he would not have been able to understand the love in them without letting go of his own broken image of fatherhood and loss.

King Jesus motioned to an angel standing near at hand, and the robed figure stepped forward, enormous and shimmering, with a pile of garments for the King. Soberly, the One who sat upon the Throne turned to Elijah.

"We shall fit you for battle, my son," he said quietly. "We shall make you ready with all the gifts of the Kingdom, and you will stand before us for knighthood, at last, to receive the sword for which you have come so far, and with which you will fight the good fight."

As he spoke, the angels began fastening garments around Elijah. There was a strong belt about his waist that the King called "the belt of truth," meant to strengthen him as he stood in triumph. There was righteousness, the protective armor that covered his heart, and footwear that strapped firmly around his ankles so that he would be alert and willing to share in the blessings of peace. As each garment was strapped and buckled into place, Elijah felt the strength of the room gathering about him. He saw in the corner of his vision that the angels, the beasts, the saints, and all others in the Throne Room had paused in what they were doing and were gathering to watch with interest all that was taking place on the dais.

"This is your shield of faith," the King said, holding out a great shield with curved, gilt edges. "It is your wrap-around faith, able to extinguish the blazing arrows of the Dark One. And here is your helmet of salvation, to protect your thoughts from lies along the way."

The King paused, and in his holy silence, a hush rippled through the Throne Room. Then he turned and retrieved a great, gleaming sword from behind him. Elijah recognized that sword at once--it was the same one he had caught glimpses of in the Chamber of Wisdom, but now it was unsheathed before him in splendor, and it filled him with raw excitement. This was the Sword of the Spirit forged by the Spirit, the truth of the Word of God, a shimmering blade, and the length and breadth of it spoke of great adventure ahead.

"Are you ready to receive the mantle of knighthood in my Kingdom?" the King asked.

Elijah bowed his head and sank to one knee in wordless response, and the King reached out with the tip of the sword, touching it gracefully to Elijah's shoulders and then to his head.

"Go forth, then," he said. "Fight the good fight and enter into the battle with prayer and thanksgiving. We shall sing the song of the Lord, and that song will resonate in your heart from this day forward."

Even as he spoke, the crowd all around began to lift their voices in worship. The song was so sweet and so lovely that Elijah felt his eyes filling with tears, and yet he could hear the undercurrent of preparation in it, the rhythm of the drums of purpose and battle. He took the sword the King offered him and sheathed it, comforted by the weight against his leg. Overjoyed, King Jesus spoke to Elijah and said, "I will be with you. I will never forsake you, Mighty Warrior."

With this, Elijah's heart increased with love, his mind began to be filled with the thoughts of Christ, "Is my mind becoming like yours? Is my heart being filled with your love?" Elijah asked Jesus.

"Yes, my son," Jesus said.

"And the song, this sound filling the Throne Room," Elijah asked. "What does it mean? Should I not be preparing for the fight with the Dark One now that I have been knighted at last?"

"This is your preparation," King Jesus said, smiling over the crowd of joyous people. "They know what you will soon learn-- worship lays a path for victory. They are going out before you, preparing the way for the battle you will fight. Worship and praise are not background or warm-up for real spiritual life.

They are spiritual life. Even now, the Enemy quakes at the sound of Heaven."

The music swelled, and Elijah thought fleetingly of all the times when he had prepared for fights, of the roar of the crowd and the intensity of the ring ahead of him. None of that compared with the adrenaline and purpose of this moment. He looked out over the faces of those who knew that he had been commissioned by the King and remembered with joy that those who are commissioned by the King can walk in His Strength and Wisdom.

He raised his own voice in praise and lost himself in the worship of the moment. He had no idea how long he stood this way, with his eyes turned towards the King, but he was shaken from his reverie by the hand of the Warrior of Old on his arm.

"It is time," the Warrior of Old said. "The battle has begun."

Chapter Thirteen

The Battle

The room all around Elijah began to fill with smoke--not a frightening, choking smoke, but a holy presence that wrapped around Elijah like the wind. The sound of praise was all around him, and the glory of the smoke-filled his heart. He could see nothing at first, and then the fog became clear until only a few wisps remained.

He was no longer in the Throne Room. He was no longer even in the castle. He recognized the wooded land as the same forest he had run through when he was first fleeing to safety: full of dark shapes and shadows. He looked around him, but he was alone for the first time since he had come to the castle. The Warrior of Old was nowhere to be seen, nor was the King at his side or any of the other people he had met along the way.

He felt a chill of fear remembering the dark forces that had chased him to the castle in the first place, and took one or two steps forward, trying to gather his thoughts. It seemed impossible that the same glorious King who moments ago had knighted him, outfitted him with armor, and prepared him for a battle, should now abandon him, but Elijah felt alone, nonetheless.

He took a few steps forward because it was the only thing he knew how to do, and no sooner had he started down the road, but a figure appeared on the trail ahead. Elijah slowed his step and dropped his hand to the sword at his side.

"Who is there?" he called into the darkness.

The man ahead came forward with a light in his hands. When he drew near, Elijah felt himself relax. The man was overwhelmingly ordinary, and the light in his hands was a small lantern. He was the first person in this strange and foreign land that was not dressed for battle. He was wearing a long fur robe the same color as the green forest all around, and this garment was belted at the waist with a wide strip of festive silk. He had an almost cheerful face and a flowing brown beard. Elijah was instantly at ease around him. His eyes were open and calm, his manner relaxed.

"Hello friend," he said, not offering his name. "I was just starting along this path myself. Would you like company for the journey?"

Elijah turned back towards the castle. What he really wanted was the Warrior of Old to appear again at his side, but after a long moment of silence, the castle walls only stared back at him blankly. Some company seemed better than none.

Elijah turned back with a smile, but something still told him to keep his hand on his sword. He did so, approaching the man in the path. "I could do with a friend tonight," he said.

"Where are you going?" the man asked.

Elijah wasn't sure how to answer that. The battle? It seemed vague and almost silly to speak of such things in this man's company. Instead, he answered honestly. "I am to walk along this path for a time," he said. "I will know my destination when I meet it."

The man shrugged. "Good enough for me," he said. "But I have a destination, and it is worth looking forward to. Would you like me to tell you about it as we walk?"

"By all means."

They began to walk, and a brisk pace down the forest path. The lantern in the man's hand kept the way lit before them, but it made the shadows longer on every side. The darkness was intimidating enough, but the lantern made every tree and bush look as though it was moving, and Elijah found himself looking around, again and again, to be sure they weren't being followed by the Dark One or his forces. His companion, however, seemed at ease. He kept talking about the place where he was going and what he meant to do there.

"It is a beautiful pasture," he said. "The land is beautiful and peaceful, and there is always light. You will see when we come to it--the sunlight beckons from far away. There are streams there and quiet places, and things to occupy your time that are delightfully entertaining. The people are polite and good, proper and kind when necessary. You will want to join me when you see it, I assure you."

The words sounded inviting, and yet Elijah couldn't be confident of them. It wasn't that anything about the man was explicitly wrong--he seemed very smart and reasonable. He had a broad smile and a precise manner and spoke about the place he wanted to go enticingly. Yet something didn't fit. He realized that while nothing the man said was wrong, there was also nothing about the man that reminded Elijah of the castle or the King. He spoke about peace and order and civility, but in the castle, Elijah had fought alongside the Warrior of Old to destroy the idols in his life, he had learned about the passion of the King, and he had prepared for a battle. There had been no talk about how to live a polite life in the company of courteous people.

At last, the two came to a fork in the road, and just as the man had described, Elijah saw a bit of light coming through the trees to the left, and the path leading there was lush with curling greener. It seemed soft and inviting. The road to the right was darker than anything he had walked on yet, and, worse than that, Elijah knew without being told that the road to his right was the road to the battle. He shuddered and wavered.

"This is where I turn off," the man said cheerily. "Won't you consider coming with me? I tell you, there is nothing but pain down that other road, and the place where I am going is almost like Heaven. It's a dream."

Elijah had been coming to an understanding of his companion the entire walk, but that phrase--it's a dream--was the last straw. He had been offered a dream before when he returned from the war. He had achieved an excellent job and a house with a picket-fence, and it had been emptiness. He had done all that because he was afraid of facing his own demons.

He took a step back from the man at his side.

"No," he said, keeping an even tone. The man's placid face seemed suddenly terrifying. "I will walk on. My trail lies to the right; I know it."

The man did not give in, however. He smiled slowly. "It is very dangerous. What I am offering is as easy as a single step to the left, and the rest will come to you without you even having to try."

Yes, Elijah had learned that the hard way. He had slipped into an empty life, not even seeking one. "No," he said, trying to remember the castle and the lessons he had learned.

"Why not?" the man asked, his voice low and musical. Something had shifted in the atmosphere. Elijah felt as though the green path to the left was no longer just a path--it was drawing him towards it, warm and inviting, or perhaps the man was drawing him. He tried to step back and couldn't.

"I have to go," he said weakly. His voice lacked conviction.

"Why?" The man tilted his head to the side, a smile on his lips. "I have offered you something far better, and you are choosing the harder way."

It was harder. As if on cue, a gust of cold air came from the path to the right. Elijah realized that he was trying to walk away from the other man, but not a single muscle responded: he was frozen. The castle seemed very far away.

"I can't." The words were almost a surrender.

Again, the man asked his simple question. "Why not?"

Elijah felt desperate. He felt he had to answer the man, but he could think of nothing, and so he spoke aloud as though the Warrior of Old were still standing by his side. "Why not?" he repeated.

At once, he felt a chill along his arms, and a voice spoke in his head as clearly as if the Warrior of Old was standing with him. Do not partner with fear. It is a foe dressed up as a friend on the road to battle. He claims it is an alternative route to peace, but it is a road to destruction. Jesus' Kingdom does not reside in the pasture of compromise. Elijah looked up, confidence filling him. He had not been left alone, after all. The Warrior was still with him. He looked at the man across from him.

"I have gone that way before," he said. "I know that in the land you seek, I will not have to take any stance or fight any battle. That way holds the illusion of safety, but it is anything but safe." He shook his head.

He turned and began walking down the path towards where he knew the battle waited. He heard nothing at all behind him. It was as though the man disappeared entirely for a time, and Elijah resisted every urge to turn and be sure he was not being followed.

The path he walked upon now was far narrower, and there were branches at places that arched over the road so that he had to duck and climb more than walk. When he, at last, pushed through into a clearing, he stopped short in surprise. The path opened like a gash in the trees, and the blackness of the forest was dispelled by a beautiful yet eerie scene. There was a wide valley before him, illuminated by a full, steel moon flooding the arena with silver light. The valley was completely empty except for thick fog, but Elijah could feel a heavy presence there.

After all, he was trained for moments like these. He could feel what he had felt a hundred times, what many calls the calm before the storm. Still, this was different than any of his deployments. Time seemed to be frozen, yet he could almost taste the past, present, and future: as though this very moment would last until the end of time. It reminded Elijah of the rivers in the Throne Room, fully present and yet full of eternity.

A wind picked at his clothes, howling up to the promontory where he was standing, and the trees near him wailed as though the Earth was crying out. There was movement in the valley.

Elijah saw the topography in motion as the grass shifted with the wind like ocean waves. It was beautiful but terrifying. There was a promise here of a better day, but Elijah could feel the darkness threatening that promise. It undermined the hope he felt and crawled along his spine. Elijah knew without asking that this valley was a place of decision upon which the world, perhaps even the universe, hung in the balance.

Across the valley in the distance, Elijah made out seven dark mountains. Elijah felt dark forces surrounding each peak, as though there was a demonic characteristic for each.

He knew that these evil mountains had a significant influence on mankind on the Earth but knew he required a higher understanding of wisdom and strength to withstand these evil principalities' works.

I am always with you. It was the Warrior of Old again.

Relieved to hear the voice of his friend, Elijah strained his eyes to peer through the fog in the valley. "Where is the battle?" he asked.

Close your eyes and listen.

Elijah closed his eyes to a sound, distant at first and then so close and overwhelming that he had to catch his breath in alarm: it was the sound of metal against metal, the clanging of swords and shields. He also heard pain, suffering, the sounds of death. The smell of burning sulfur filled his nostrils, mingled with the scent of war. Elijah was a soldier. He knew those sounds and smells all too well. Still, the valley appeared empty.

He listened closely and noticed differences in the clanging and crashing sounds. The pitches were different, and depending on the sound that came to his ears, Elijah felt hope or despair. Some of the sounds were so pure he wanted to open his eyes and rejoice, while some were so dark that he had to fight the urge to retreat. "They sound different," he said aloud, speaking to the Warrior of Old. "Each sword has its own sound."

They sound differently based upon how the metal of the weapon was forged. Even iron testifies righteousness or death.

The Warrior of Old continued. Now open your eyes, my son. It is upon you.

Elijah turned, and before him, the scene transformed by degrees, as though a wave of revelation was washing over it from one end to the other. The wind that he had felt all around him a moment before seemed to be painting the landscape. With each pass, things became more apparent. At first, there were only shadows, then the flash of silver. Across the vast expanse, he saw the battle that he had only felt before. The sight of it made his blood run cold.

The armies arrayed against the people of God were darker than he had ever imagined, filling the valley with a heaviness. There were the screeching and clashing of screams and weapons, the smell of sulfur all around, and the occasional glint of a sword in the moonlight. Overhead, swooping bat-like creatures dove again and again into the chaos. Screams came whenever they landed. It was ghastly, and Elijah fell back with memories of his own deployments pressing down on him.

"There are so many of them," he said aloud.

As the words came out of his mouth, he turned and looked behind him for the first time. The man from the trail was standing there at the mouth of the forest. The man was still a few yards off, but there was something different about him now, and as he walked towards Elijah, he mimicked the words that the Warrior of Old had spoken in his heart only a few moments before.

"I will always be here," he said.

Elijah took hold of his sword. "I know who you are," he said, planting his feet even though his knees were shaking beneath him. "You are Fear, and you have come again to dissuade me from the fight."

"If you know me so well, then there is no more need for this paltry disguise," the man said. He threw off the long green robe and dropped to his knees. When he raised his head again, the sight was grotesque. Fear still had a man's shape but was scaly and monstrous, with wings coming from his back. He trotted forward on all fours, half leaping and half walking, laughing in a way that made Elijah's spine shiver. "Do you see how many people are on my side?" he said, his voice mocking. "They always come ready to fight, they never weary, and they are winning."

Elijah turned and looked again at the valley. It looked to him as though Fear was right. The valley was swarming with the Enemy like locusts devouring a field. He couldn't make out the Enemy's opposition, but they did not seem to be very successful. The darkness was like ink, staining the valley and the world around. He wanted to run back up the trail, but then he thought of the Warrior of Old and stood his ground.

"You do not have the right to speak to me," he said to Fear. "I have no need of you here."

"Who else will point out to you the obvious?" Fear said, laughing, his yellow eyes flitting to the battle and back. "Who else will show you that this is all a hopeless fight that you will never win?"

"You lie," Elijah said, and even as he spoke, he felt the truth of the statement echoed by the Warrior of Old in his heart. "You always lie."

Fear slowed. "You will never succeed. Think about poor Charlie. You'll end up like him one day if you keep fighting." He clicked his tongue as though chiding Elijah. "Poor little Eli, destined to follow in the same path, are we?"

Elijah blinked. His vision seemed suddenly clear. "My name is not Eli any longer," he said. "I'm called Elijah now, and I fight for the true King."

Elijah wasn't sure that he could win the battle spread out below him. He wasn't even sure he could win a battle against this sniveling creature, but he was done being afraid. He wanted to fight again, and he wanted to fight for something worthy. He looked at the beast in front of him and knew he would never be able to do battle in the company of Fear. He drew his sword and swiped at the creature with a decisive blow. He was more successful than he deserved to be, for the first cut was not very strong and didn't show much finesse. Still, Fear clearly had not expected it and took the brunt of the blow on his right arm. He fell back, squealing, and suddenly seemed smaller than he had a moment before. Elijah advanced, expecting Fear to retaliate, but the thing only writhed about in a fury for a moment before limping quickly off into the woods again.

"Fear is a coward," came a voice at Elijah's side.

He whirled, sword drawn, but it was not another enemy. The Warrior of Old was standing beside him, and when he saw Elijah, he smiled a slow, intense smile. He was no longer in the long robes that he had worn for the entirety of their journey through the castle. He was dressed in armor just as Elijah was, and his long white hair was braided back away from his face. He had a sword at his side and a steel glint in his eye.

Elijah resisted the urge to throw himself into the Warrior of Old's arms. Instead, he bowed his head respectfully.

"You took your time coming to the battle," he said with a smile.

"I was with you," the Warrior of Old answered with a smile of his own. "And you did well."

Elijah looked at the place where Fear had disappeared. "I suppose he is gone for good now?"

The Warrior laughed drily, and the sound seemed impossibly out of place with the battle raging near at hand. "Fear is not resilient, but he returns again and again whenever he sees an opening. Be careful not to partner with him. He seems harmless enough, but he feeds on a man like a leech."

Elijah took a deep, shaking breath and wiped the dark blood of the beast off his sword. He straightened and looked out at the battle raging below. Just then, the dark skies lit up with what seemed thousands of fiery arrows illuminating the valley below.

"Where should we join the fight?" Elijah asked, fighting

discouragement.

The Warrior of Old came to stand at his side and put a reassuring hand on Elijah's shoulder. He extended His other arm to indicate portions of the field spread out below them.

"Look there by the trees in the center of the valley," he said. "Do you see the creatures there?"

Elijah sucked in his breath. It would have been hard to miss them beneath the flames: the demons looked like giants compared to the rest of the field and were attacking the slight figures before them with bulky, destructive swings of their clubs. "I do."

"Look closer, through the smoky fog, and you will see the deception. It's part of the demonic strategy."

The Warrior of Old then turned to another part of the field, and Elijah saw the battle for justice reflected not only in a tangle of swords and blows but in the faces of children and the murder of innocents. Another portion of the valley showed a slow singular force rippling like a black river over those fighting against it. The Warrior of Old showed Elijah that it was the spirits of death and disease, an overpowering force that swallowed up the few fighters taking a stand against it.

There was a line of trebuchets constructed with large cedars of petrified wood and fallen warriors' bones on the far hill. The machines of war were operated by troll-like creatures who were all the more hideous for ways they resembled humanity. They loaded stone after stone into the machines and hurled them relentlessly to the battle below. They threw without precision, and there was a shrill scraping sound accompanying the throws.

Elijah realized it was the sound of demon laughter and shivered. The Warrior of Old saw where Elijah was looking and sighed. "Chaos," he said. "A favorite weapon of the Enemy."

Elijah looked more closely at the battles. "There are men on the battlefield," he said startled. "I can see them. They aren't just fighting against the Enemy; some men are fighting alongside the darkness." And there it was. As Elijah looked closer at each battle scene, he could see that this theater encompassed all war, including the final battle.

As a sniper, Elijah had studied historical battles, strategic movement, and battle flow. He had trained to make informed decisions as he approached any battlefield. Here before him, he saw the most impressive battle of all time with the elements of war throughout the centuries woven through it like a tapestry. He recognized the invasions of the Vikings, the Crusades, and the Mongols. He saw guerilla warfare, armored advances, and slinking lines of endless infantry crawling along with various places in the wide field.

He could see clearly man's plight and how the dark forces had operated through all this bloodshed. As Elijah looked, he was reminded of how the martyrs had seemed in the Throne Room-- when he saw their faces and simultaneously their past and present. Here, he saw the battle directly before him but felt he could also see what the giants were fighting for and how the demonic deception played out on Earth. He saw that the mass by the trees was a battle over physical violence and watched in horror as it rippled out across the nations: on the mountains of Afghanistan, in city allies and streets with looting and fire, in government corruption, in company back offices, in hospital emergency rooms, in chaotic homes between a husband and a wife.

The Warrior of Old nodded soberly.

"Mankind does not always see the battle as clearly as you do," he said. "They have agreed with the deception and are perpetuating the demonic agenda on Earth." He smiled. "But the demonic forces are not the only ones with whom man can partner, Elijah. Look closely at those fighting back."

Elijah looked and saw that there were humans on the side of light as well.

"Why are some warriors battered and exhausted, yet others have endless strength and wisdom?" asked Elijah.

"These warriors are waiting on the Lord, and their strength and wisdom are being renewed by Him. They do not do battle in their own power. They do not turn to their own desires. Instead, they are using the weapons the Lord is providing. The weapons of prayer, the declaration of truth, and the weapons of praise, worship, fasting, anointings, and the gifts and the fruit of the spirit." The old man smiled. "They have the same armor you do, and victory comes to these warriors. They appear to be soaring on the wings of eagles, they run and not grow weary, and they walk and are never tired, never grow faint."

Still, with all there was to examine and learn, Elijah found his eyes drawn again and again to a particular area of the valley where there was only a dark shadow. He saw the occasional glint of a sword and the movement of darkness within darkness, but there seemed to be little battle going on.

"What is there?" he asked.

The Warrior of Old turned and looked at him, eyes like fire. "That is why you are here," he said. "The King will tell you of your calling."

"Where is the King?" Elijah asked the question that had been in his heart all along. "If he comes, he should come soon. We look to be losing this battle."

The Warrior of Old smiled, and then his eyes slid closed, and he said aloud, "Open his eyes."

The first thing Elijah saw was the castle on a far hilltop. It must have been there all along, but he had not noticed it until that moment. It looked like a city on a hill, shining light forth and down into the dark valley.

There were seven lampstands on seven tower points on the walls of the fortress. It represented a beacon of hope and a reminder of the victory we have with the King. Elijah felt the stiff wind that had been wailing around him shift all at once in the opposite direction--firm but gentle and warm now. The castle was silhouetted against the sunrise breaking behind it, and Elijah saw shapes begin to emerge from the blinding light: thousands upon thousands of profiles. It was "the" Army, and at the head was the King.

He knew Him at once--Jesus riding in on a great white horse with the four creatures from the Throne Room at his side and a wave of angels behind him. They were a diverse force, some riding, some flying, some running forward with great and bounding leaps to meet the demons, evil men, giants, and monstrous entities in the valley below. Just moments before, the demon force had seemed endless, but now Elijah could see that the heavenly armies outnumbered them in a vast array of light and power. The sunrise filled the valley, and the armies poured in like a wave, crashing against the forces below.

"Victory will be swift," he said, his eyes full of tears. "The forces of darkness will have to bend their knee--it is a wonder they continue to fight at all instead of fleeing in fear."

The Warrior of Old turned a sober expression to Elijah. "It is well that you should think so, for a day will come when evil will be defeated forever, but this is not that day--the battle rages on."

"How?" Elijah asked. "It is impossible that the dark forces could stand their ground against this."

He was answered not by the Warrior of Old, but by another familiar, beloved voice. The King himself had come to stand beside them on the promontory. He sat upon his white horse, the warm wind lifting his billowing robes about him, and watched the battle with eyes of steel.

"I came to die for all men," he said. "I came to save them all, and I honor every man's right to choose me for himself. Some do not see me because of deception, some do not see me because of greed, and some choose evil."

"I don't understand," Elijah said his voice breaking. "Why would you let them choose something so terrible?"

"If they cannot choose something terrible, then they also cannot choose Me, my son. There is no true love without the free will of choice." He turned his eyes to Elijah, that were full of sadness. "It is as it was in the beginning. I gave Adam authority over the Earth, and he handed that authority to the serpent. To this day, mankind continues to give over their authority in the Kingdom to the darkness."

Elijah looked out on the vast expanse and saw that there were indeed places where the darkness was standing its ground.

Jesus climbed down from his horse. The creature walked behind him in devoted deference as he approached Elijah. Jesus' nearness was overpowering, and Elijah found himself sinking to his knees.

"Stand, my son," the King said, helping to lift Elijah to his feet. He took him by the shoulders in tenderness and then turned so that they were both looking again at the shadowed portion of the battle. "It is here that I have called you," he said. "On Earth, death comes prematurely for my earthly warriors, whether in battle or in despair, and it is here that the fight happens hour by hour in the hearts of my children. You cannot see it on the surface, just as it is nearly still here, but beneath the cloud, there is a desperate battle against deception and despair."

Elijah turned and saw the King's eyes were full of tears. Jesus turned to him and spoke in a broken voice. "I know Charlie, my son."

Elijah felt his handshake with fear on the hilt of his sword. "No," he said. "This cannot be my calling. I am not strong enough for it. All my life, I have been fighting these spirits of despair and their weapons of suicide through night terrors--how can I fight it in the heart of others?" He looked again upon the twisted darkness below and shook his head. "I will lose."

The King stretched out his arm to the golden armies streaming down. They looked as if they were riding on the rays of the sun to the battle.

"They are fighting for you when you do not even know to ask

for their aid," he said. "My son, upon your knighting, you have been grafted into the Kingdom, apart from Me, there is only loss, but with Me, there is only victory. They will go with you now, and this is what you will bring back to my sons and daughters suffering in the shadow." His voice was gentle but urgent. "You know that no matter how dark the battle may seem, the heavenly hosts are waging war alongside you. You know the pain of despair, but you also know that the victory is sure."

The Warrior of Old came and lifted Elijah's right arm for Elijah to see the side of his sword.

"My son, look upon your sword and read what is engraved."

Elijah looked and saw: My Grace and Love are your Strength and Wisdom when you kneel at My Throne.

King Jesus added, "This is my promise to you."

The Warrior of Old smiled at Elijah. "Come boldly unto the Throne of grace, that you may obtain mercy, and find grace to help in time of need. Seek first the Kingdom and Righteousness, and everything will be provided for you for this mission. You are to always come to the Three Chambers in your heart, my son. The Chamber of Strength, the Chamber of Wisdom, and the Throne Room are to be surrendered daily. I know the hope that is before you and shares this hope in the wisdom given to you. You can then display His immeasurable greatness and his Strength according to the working of the King's great wisdom and power as you conquer the Enemy and fight for the saints that may not know the King as you do. You saw how the sword was forged with fire and a hammer, and in that way, you have and will be forged by the pressures ahead."

"Do not despair," the King added. "Each step builds upon the next, and you will be prepared for the purpose and destiny assigned to you by God. You will have everything you require at the moment when you need it. The Spirit of the Lord, of wisdom and understanding and counsel and strength and knowledge and fear of the Lord, will be upon you."

Elijah looked down at the shadow again. Light from the heavenly forces descending on the battle showed him glimpses of dark and twisted creatures through the dense covering, but he also saw the people battling there: the intercessors weeping for those held captive by the Enemy. He drew his sword.

"Here I am," he said with reserved confidence. "Send me."

The King said, "Go then, my son, with the one who guides you well." He drew the Warrior of Old forward. "Your companion on your journey thus far will not leave your side when you step into the battle. You have met me, and because of me, you know my father--now you shall have the Holy Spirit with you as well."

"You?" Elijah turned to the Warrior of Old, who had guided him along the entirety of the journey thus far. "You are the Holy Spirit?" He had heard Daniel speak from the pulpit before about the power of the Holy Spirit, but it had always seemed to him a vague ally to have in life. There was nothing vague about the Warrior who had fought alongside him through this adventure and who was now walking into battle with him, shoulder to shoulder like a brother. Elijah reached out, and with the desperation of a lost child, returned at last to his Father and embraced the Holy Spirit. "Thank you," he said.

The two turned once more to the King. The Warrior of Old took out a vial of oil and poured it over Elijah's head. King Jesus then stretched out His left hand and blessed Elijah on his forehead, and with His right hand, He handed Elijah a coin.

Elijah took the coin and read the inscriptions on each side. "I will always be with you Mighty Warrior," ad "My Grace and Love are your Strength and Wisdom when you kneel at My Throne."

Elijah, grateful and believing in the promise, started off into the darkness of the valley with the Warrior of Old--the Holy Spirit--charging at his side. Elijah felt no fear--even as the dark shapes before him grew more and more ominous. He felt his soul swelling with the praise of the Throne Room and the knowledge that the armies against him were nothing compared to the heavenly hosts coming to his aid.

As he ran, the light of shining hosts grew brighter and brighter until his vision was full of radiance. He saw a creature of darkness coming towards him like a shadow with a sword raised, dark and twisted. He raised his own sword and swung it hard. The clanging of the two blades clashing rang in his ears.

It echoed, again and again, a steady sound in the bright whiteness of the light all around him. Elijah listened to it, gripping his sword and waiting for the creature to strike again, but as he listened, he realized it wasn't the sound of metal at all but a sort of steady alarm beeping over and over again in his ear.

Suddenly everything went dark. He felt the urge to open his eyes and did so, not remembering when he had closed them. The battlefield's sounds died away, and the smell of desperation and purpose was replaced by the bitter scent of disinfectant. He knew this place from another life. There was a bright light overhead. It took a moment for his eyes to adjust. The sound of the sword in the valley had shifted, and he now knew the beeping for what it was: a hospital monitor.

Chapter Fourteen

Life After

Elijah blinked, and everything rushed back to him--the fight with Draxler, the blow to his head, and then everything that followed.

He didn't even think to wonder whether or not it had all been a dream because the reality of the vision he had experienced was still all over him like the smoke in the Throne Room. He could still feel the praise echoing through his body, even over the ache in his head and neck. His hand twitched at his side, and he realized he was still reaching for his sword though there was nothing at his side now.

He thought of Sarah and turned to look to his side. The room was small and white, divided by a curtain, and by the far wall, he saw Daniel, Eric, and John engaged in quiet conversation. Elijah tried to speak, but at first, only a mumble came out. It was enough. All three men turned in astonishment.

"Eli?" Daniel rose and came to his side, putting a hand on his. "Did you say something?"

"His eyes are open," John said, with Eric coming near as well.

Elijah nodded weakly, licking his dry lips. He looked to the water cup sitting beside the bed, and Daniel understood at once, fetching it for him. Elijah drank, remembering the water of life Jesus had shown him in the well. When he finished, he could speak.

"Sarah?" he said.

Daniel was at his side. "Sarah should be back any minute big man. She's been here for days by your side. How are you feeling?"

"Days?" Elijah could barely speak.

"Yeah, bud, you've been out for a few. Sarah took Mary and Jeffrey home to get the little guy fed and in bed. She was going to shower and change, but she should be back any minute." Tears started into Daniel's eyes. "I'm glad to have you back, bro."

"You've been out for a week and a half," John added. "We've all been praying."

Elijah saw the worry in their eyes and pushed back the guilt that rose inside him at the memory of who he had been. That was behind him now--the castle and the King had shown him that there were more important things to live for. He reached forward, urgent, and caught Daniel's hand.

"I'm in the Kingdom," he said.

Daniel blinked, taken aback. "What did you say?"

"I said I am in the Kingdom," he felt hot tears welling in his eyes. "I met the King."

Daniel's face transformed before him into quiet joy. "King Jesus?" he asked softly.

Elijah smiled, tears running down his cheeks, and nodded wordlessly. There were no more words, not now at least. There would be a time when he would share with Daniel all that he had been taught when he would tell him about their father and about forgiveness and about the sword he had been given. For now, it was enough that they were brothers together in the Kingdom, and that Daniel understood that.

Elijah's gaze shifted to John and Eric, who were stepping back to give the brothers a moment alone together.

"Wait," he said.

John and Eric stopped. John said, "Yeah, buddy?"

"I'm so sorry. I'm grateful for you guys, so much to tell you."

Eric smiled gently. "Absolutely, son. We love you; there will be plenty of time. We are just so happy you are back. You gave us quite a scare."

A quiet shuffling sound came from the door, and Sarah slipped into the room in a sweatshirt and jeans, her hair in a loose bun, her face weary. Elijah felt a pang of regret at the sight of her worry, and yet he also felt drawn to her as he hadn't felt in years.

She froze when she saw him awake and put a small hand to her mouth.

John nodded to Eric and touched Daniel's elbow. "We'll give you a moment alone," he said.

Daniel squeezed Elijah's hand once more. "Love you, brother, can't wait to catch up." The three men slipped out of the room.

"Eli?" She came over to his bed, sinking down into the chair and taking his hand in hers.

His eyes were heavy, and his hand weak, but he lifted both to her. "Sarah, I'm sorry."

Tears filled her eyes. She leaned over and put her hand on his face. "We didn't know if you'd wake up. We kept waiting and praying, but we didn't know. The doctor said it was a hard hit..."

"I'm sorry," he repeated. The first time he hadn't even been thinking about the way she'd likely heard about his accident or how angry she would be about his fighting--he'd just been thinking of how distant he had been before and how she deserved so much better. "I wasn't there for you," he said. His hand was weak, but he squeezed hers as hard as he could. "I'll be there for you now."

She looked at him in confusion, but he could see that she was happy. "You should rest," she said. "I should call for the nurse. They'll want to do tests. They didn't think you would wake up."

"Just stay here with me," he said, holding on to her. "You can call for the nurse in a minute."

She lay her head down on the bedspread, holding his arm like a lifeline, and he reached his other hand over to gently stroke her hair. He heard the rhythmic promise of the Warrior of Old, like a heartbeat in his mind: I will always be with you.

"Of all the things He has given me, you are the dearest," he said quietly.

She raised her eyes to his, confusion and happiness mixed on her face.

He swallowed hard. "I know I don't usually talk like that, but I mean to. I don't want you to ever doubt the way I feel about you."

She smiled. "You don't usually talk about Him either," she said. She paused a moment and then added softly. "I'm glad you came back to us. I...I have news. I had been waiting to surprise you, but then this happened...I thought I would never be able to tell you."

Her hand slid down to rest gently on her stomach for the briefest of moments. It was a tiny gesture, but Elijah understood it immediately. It was hope; it was another second chance.

***

The doctors came in and out of the room, and the nurses followed with tests and questions and food, but it all blurred together. No one knew how he had come out of the coma so quickly or so whole, but the matter seemed small to Elijah. The reality of all that he had experienced was still far greater to him, and he lay in bed through it all, looking at Sarah and praying in his heart to the Warrior and to the King.

At long last, he convinced Sarah to go home for the night. Daniel was planning on sitting vigil later in the evening, and he knew he would only be alone for a few hours. She relented but made him promise to answer his cell if she called. He tucked it at his side and lay back with his eyes closed, thinking about the battle and the shadow in the valley.

He hadn't even fallen asleep when he heard the nurse come in to check on the patient across the curtain from him. He listened as she talked to the man and heard the man respond in short, curt phrases. When the nurse had gone, Elijah closed turned to sleep again, but before he did, he heard the Warrior in his head, gentle and pressing love him.

Elijah didn't hesitate. He spoke through the curtain. "I suppose if we are to share a room together, we should at least be introduced," he said.

There was a long silence, and then the man's gruff voice replied, "I didn't know you were awake." He gave a dry laugh. "I mean, everyone knows you're awake--the miracle kid and all that--I just meant I thought you were resting."

"I'm Elijah."

"Yikes," the man answered. "That must have been a tough name to have in middle school."

"I went by Eli," Elijah answered, smiling to himself. "And you are?"

"Not interested in a friend," the man answered.

Elijah waited. Love him. "Good," he said after a moment. "Because I'm not interviewing for the position of friend, just hospital roommate."

The man gave a short, gruff laugh. "You remind me of a guy I used to know," he said. "He was always cracking jokes--never met a person he didn't like."

Elijah hid a smile, thinking of who he had been before the King found him. Eli had met many people he didn't like, but Elijah was a new creation, and he only had one Enemy to watch for now.

"This buddy of yours, did he always wake up from a coma?" he asked.

"Negative," the man answered, his voice suddenly dull. "IED, in the Sandbox."

Elijah felt a jolt of Holy Spirit revelation. "Army. What branch were you?"

"Iraq. 3rd Battalion 25th Marines, Lucky Lima." Of course, the man sharing a room with him would be a veteran. Elijah waited. I'm sorry. "I'm sorry," he said after the words came to him. "I lost friends too. Kandahar. 1st Battalion Special Forces with Rusty."

"Lions? A bunch of Meat Eaters." He heard respect in the other man's voice.

"Roger that." Elijah paused. "My brothers," he said softly.

There was a long silence, but the curtain between them seemed a little frailer. "I'm in for an overdose," the man said after a long pause. Elijah realized the curtain was a gift from God to loosen the man's tongue. He was honest because he felt safe. "I wanted it to be over with, but I miscalculated."

"I know the feeling." Elijah felt a tear come out from under his eyelid. It rolled down his cheeks, hot and freeing. He took a deep breath. "Hey, man--you got anything going on right now?"

The man on the other side of the curtain waited a long moment and then sighed. "I'll be here for another day at least, then a mental eval is in place. You know the drill."

Elijah felt a small object in his hand. Looking quickly down, he saw a coin that had not been there a moment before. "Wait, what?" Elijah thought. "No way." It wasn't just a coin; it was THE coin. Elijah felt the presence of the King again as if standing next to him. He shook his head in disbelief and smiled to himself. And as a man who discovered the secret of life but lacked the faculties to describe it in words, he attempted to formulate the revelation, nonetheless.

"Man," he said softly, "Mind if I tell you a story?"

Made in the USA
Coppell, TX
21 December 2020